HOPE, FAITH, AND COURAGE

AMISH FAMILY AND FAITH

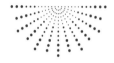

SARAH MILLER

D1523219

SWEETBOOKHUB.COM

WELCOME TO THE FAMILY OF FAITH'S CREEK

I started sharing my stories of the Amish of Faith's Creek back in December 2014. Since then I have had a lot of readers asking me for details about what happened to certain characters. The couple that is asked about the most is Anna and Samuel Miller.

They first came to Life in Amish Baby Hope. A story about their struggles in life and how they vanish when we concentrate on what is important. I never wrote the story of Anna and Samuel's courtship but now it can be found in *Anna's Amish Season*.

I then decided to look at the other stories I've been asked about and add more bits to them. You may have already read some of the books in this series but they have been updated. To end the series I have a new book coming featuring Hope called, Hope, Faith, and Courage. I hope you enjoy them all.

Sarah

The books in this series:

Anna's Amish Season - A New Book

Mary's Faith - Updated and Extended Version

Hanna's Journey Home - Updated and Extended Version

Katie's Amish Choice - Updated and Extended Version

Amish Baby Hope - Updated and Extended Version

Hope Faith and Courage - A New Book

If you are not already a member, why not join Sarah's Newsletter here. She will share with you her books and those from authors she likes to read. You will be the first to learn of any new releases and will receive occasional free stories.

CHAPTER ONE

* * *

He heals the brokenhearted and binds up their wounds.
Psalm 147:3

* * *

Hope Miller put down the ax and stretched her back. She was not tired, but it gave her an excuse to stare across the field at a handsome young man with thick dark hair working a team of chestnut Dutch draft horses. The big, gentle beasts turned in perfect harmony, making light work of maneuvering the heavy plow over the fertile ground and laying it ready for planting.

Even from this distance, she thought she could see his lips moving. He would be praising the horses for a job well done. Though many in the district did not appreciate Andy Byler the way Hope did, it always pleased her how kind and generous he was to his team of horses. They loved him for it; she thought that was a *gut* thing.

Why am I watching him? The thought took her by surprise. They had been friends all their lives. But over the last six months, this was much to the annoyance of her parents and many in the district. That was the problem with being the miracle *boppli*, the one which the whole district felt a part of. So much was expected of her, too much.

Andy had been well-liked, but he had gotten into a bit of trouble on his *rumspringa*, which had not gone unnoticed. Although, in many ways, it was *nee* worse than what anyone else did; unfortunately, his trouble came home with him. Who was she kidding? The trouble was much worse, but she didn't believe it was him. She couldn't. She knew that her *mamm* and *daed*, Anna and Samuel Miller, would not approve of her courting Andy. They believed he was responsible for the heinous act that got him arrested.

The problem was she wanted to court him. The more they pushed her away from him, the more she wanted to see if he was still the man she had once known. The only thing that had changed was one foolish incident, wasn't it? Surely, the Bible said that we should forgive. They had been *gut* friends, and she had enjoyed his company, but that was before the trouble. Now, he had asked to take her to service, and she thought she would like to go. Maybe, if he had taken the wrong path, she could steer him back. If he hadn't, then she could let people know. Only, she knew they would not see it this way, and her *mamm* would be disappointed. That was something she hated. Maybe Uncle Eli could help?

What was she to do?

She began to chop again; the wood wasn't really needed. It was a distraction, and it kept her away from her *mamm*, who was trying to get her to start courting. She had even suggested Simon Glick, but Hope did not even like him. The man was as arrogant as his *daed* and, in her mind, dishonest. He got into way more trouble than Andy; it was just that Simon managed to pass the blame onto others. Why did the adults never see this?

"*Gut* morning, Hope."

3

Hope looked up to see Mary Wagler walking past with her *dochder,* Lucy. "Morning." She waved.

Are you courting yet?" Mary asked.

Hope knew that this was just the way of her life. Everyone thought they were her family, all because they saved the bakery on the day she was born. But it felt like a heavy burden to carry.

Lucy winked and shrugged. Her pixie face tried to hide a grin beneath her *kapp,* and she tucked a stray lock of blonde hair back beneath it in an effort to hide her face from her *mamm.* Hope gave her a smile back and then turned to Mary. She had known Mary all her life, she was a *gut* friend of her *mamm's,* but now she felt so annoyed, not for any fault of Mary's. It was just too much pressure.

Hope is so gut; she should be courting.

Hope does everything right.

Hope can be relied upon.

Everyone loves Hope.

She had heard so much said about her, but *nee* one ever asked how she felt or what she wanted. It was stifling, and over Mary's shoulder, she watched Andy remove his hat and run a hand through his hair, and she made a decision. "*Jah*, I am. I will be riding in a courting buggy to service this Sunday."

Lucy's eyes almost popped from her head, and she whispered, "Who?"

Mary could not hear the words, but she could lip-read them.

"That is *gut*; your *mamm* must be so pleased," Mary said. "Is it Simon?"

"*Nee*, excuse me, I have to run." With that, Hope picked up an armful of the chopped wood and made her way to the *haus*.

Now she had to tell her *mamm* and to let Andy know that she was going to accept his offer.

Closing the door behind her, Hope leaned on it and let out a breath. It felt exhilarating to have done something that *nee* one would expect. But was that why she had done it? Was she simply rebelling?

She leaned against the door, still holding the wood. The *haus* was silent; of course, it was. Her *mamm* and *daed* would be next door at the bakery. They loved to bake, always had done, and still enjoyed going to work each day as much as they had done the day they started. At least, that was what they told her. It was why they had allowed her to do what she did. They believed that you must love your work, not just do something that brought in money and was a chore. Anna had loved making soap since she was a *kinner,* and she had developed it into a business. She made many different styles and fragrances, which she sold at a shop in Bird-in-Hand.

They were very sought after, especially her lavender sleep soap mix. It had sold out, and she was chopping wood to make ash to make lye to mix up the next batch. In some ways, it was like baking, so she guessed that her parents had rubbed off on her.

Moving from the door, she took the wood to the stove and stacked it in the basket next to it. There was already an ashpan with what she needed waiting there, but she had wanted to get out of the *haus* this morning when her *mamm* had begun to mention Simon Glick. Now, she realized she would have to face her *mamm* and *daed* and tell them she was courting Andy Byler.

Then panic hit her. What if Mary had gone straight to the bakery and told her *mamm?* Oh, she would be in such trouble. It was going to be bad news *nee* matter how her *mamm* heard it, but if it was from Mary! It didn't bear thinking about.

Quickly, she turned and ran out of the back door and across the ground to the bakery. Her stomach was all a flutter, and her hands were shaking. Would her *mamm* say *nee?* Would she ban her from courting Andy?

CHAPTER TWO

* * *

2 Consider it pure joy, my brothers and sisters, whenever you face trials of many kinds, 3 because you know that the testing of your faith produces perseverance. 4 Let perseverance finish its work so that you may be mature and complete, not lacking anything.

James 1:2-4

* * *

Andy bent his knees as the three big horses began to take the turn. "*Gut* job, Copper," he said to the lead horse. "Come on, Blaze and Red, you can keep up." His voice was light, and he knew the horses didn't understand his words. Still, he also knew that they understood the tone of appreciation. He had always believed that they worked better if you respected and liked them and appreciated their hard work. He always had.

A not-unpleasant prickling sensation on his arms made him look to his right. Hope had been chopping wood, and she was taking a break. Was she looking in his direction? He hoped so. It had taken all of his courage to ask her to service yesterday. He had been walking home, and she was picking sage and other herbs along the lane. Looking so pretty that she almost stopped his heart. Her cute face was concentrating so much that her tongue was poking out from between pink lips. He wanted to chuckle but had stopped himself.

He had not intended to ask, but they were getting on so well, and the words just came out. Once they did, the world seemed to stop, and he held his breath, expecting to be rejected. Only, she hadn't said *nee*, just that she must think about it.

Of course, once she had thought, she would say *nee*. What girl wouldn't? Why had he gotten into such trouble, and why hadn't he told the truth? He regretted ever going on his *rumspringa*. If he had stayed here, he might have been married to Hope by now or, at least, courting her. It was all he had ever wanted, so why had he gone away?

"Because you're a fool," he said out loud, and his voice was not as calm.

Copper's ears twitched.

"No worries, big man, I'm just telling myself off," he said in a light, almost sing-song voice. The horse's ears were forward once more.

Maybe, he could talk to Bishop Beiler and see if there was any way to repair his damaged reputation. *Jah,* that was it. The bishop may be getting old, but he would know what to do.

His eyes flicked back across the field to see Hope running into the *haus* and Mary and Lucy Wagler walking away. Had they said something to upset her? A feeling of such power welled up inside him, and he had to use all of his self-control to not drop the reins and run to her. That would not help. If she needed him, she would come and talk, but would she? Before the troubles, *jah,* she would have. But now, his reputation was that of a beast. One who was dragged home by the police for fighting. Shamed for beating a man. *Nee*, he must forget Hope.

Maybe, it was time for him to move away. As he had the thought, the sound of a bell pulled his eyes back to the farm. Old man Kanagy was ringing it to call him in from work. He looked at his watch and realized he had missed lunch. With a wave, he turned the team and headed back to the barn. It would be *gut* to rest for a while.

Once the horses were rubbed down and fed, Andy made his way to the *haus*. A sandwich and a cup of *kaffe* were waiting for him. "*Denke*," he said.

"*Ack*, you have worked hard this morning. Sit." Kanagy was in his eighties but still sprightly. Though his *fraa* died three years ago, he still had a long grey beard. But Andy noticed he was still losing weight. His trousers and shirt hung off him.

"Are you all right?" Andy asked, his own troubles forgotten.

"I'm fine. Did that lady friend of yours give you an answer yet?" Kanagy sat down and pulled his beard, his blue eyes were surrounded by wrinkles, but there was no doubting the sparkle in them.

Andy felt sad once more. "*Nee*, but I doubt she will want to be seen with me."

"Why say that? You are a *gut* lad, a *gut* worker. I will tell her for you."

Andy smiled. He had been so lucky that Marlin Kanagy had taken him in after his return. His parents were gone, they died just before he went on *rumspringa*, and he had expected to go and live with an aunt. But, instead, she had disowned him on his return, and *nee* one would offer him work. He had been about to leave the district when Kanagy had stood up and said, "If you will work the farm, there is a bed for you at my *haus*." Andy had been forever grateful.

"It is Hope Miller."

Kanagy's blue eyes widened. "*Ack*, I didn't know that, but even so, if she likes you, it will work out. So pray on it, and remember, time heals all wounds. People will forget and forgive."

"You have always been so *gut* to me; *denke, denke* so much."

Kanagy shook his head. "You have helped me, too. I could not have kept this place going without you. Why not go and speak to Amos? He will help."

"I was thinking the same thing," Andy said.

"There, you see, there is always a way to sort these things. Trust in *Gott* and trust in Amos; he will see you right."

Suddenly, Andy wanted to see Amos now, but there was still work to do; there was always work at this time of year. So he must get back to it.

"I'm sure the team will be happy for a half day off; why not go and see Amos once you have had your lunch? Mind you, save a bit of room for cake; you know how Sarah is?"

"*Denke*," Andy said and chuckled. It was true; you could not visit the bishop without his *fraa* feeding you up.

Hope walked into the front of the bakery. As always, it was busy with a mix of Amish and *Englischer* customers. Four customers were at the counter, and many were sitting at the tables, drinking *kaffe* and eating something special. The room buzzed with happy conversation. Two girls were serving on the left. Karen Schrock smiled as soon as she saw Hope and shouted behind her. Though Hope couldn't hear, she knew that she would have called to tell her *mamm* she was here.

It was just moments later when Anna came through. She ducked under the counter, and Hope saw she was carrying a tray with two cups of *kaffe* and some cookies. Her stomach started to rumble. "Hey, *Mamm*, I just thought I should tell you something. Have you seen Mary?"

"Sit. I was ready for a break, and remember, you can come in the back way to the kitchens," Anna said.

Though she knew it was not meant that way, Hope couldn't help but feel a little disappointment in the comment.

They walked across the gray tiled floor to a table in the corner. Of the eight oak tables, it was the only one empty. Hope nodded, she didn't know why, but she always felt as if she was letting her *mamm* down when she came into the shop of the bakery; however, going into the kitchens made her feel even worse. Now, here she was, about to let her down even more. How was this going to go?

Putting things off, she took a sip of the drink. The *kaffe* was hot and strong, and the cookies were white chocolate and raspberry, Hope's favorite. Taking a bite gave her even more time to think; only thinking made her worry, and now she wondered if she was doing the wrong thing. "Did Mary come to see you this morning?" she asked through a mouthful of cookie, pushing her news a little further down the road.

"*Nee*, I haven't seen her in a few days." Her *mamm's* eyebrows rose beneath her *kapp*, and worry creased the lines around her eyes. "Is she all right?"

"*Jah*, we spoke, that is all."

"What is wrong, *dochder*?" Anna asked with a smile on her freckled face.

Hope swallowed; that face was so like her own. It came with a cheeky grin and an abundance of freckles. They both tended to burn in the sun, but their eyes were always smiling. The only difference between them was age and hair color. Hope was a blonde, and her *mamm* was a brunette. Was it because they were so alike that her *mamm* knew her so well?

It didn't matter; she did. Anna could read her like a book, and she knew that worry and guilt would be plastered all over her face. "I... I..."

"Come now, I am not an ogre, whatever it is, you can tell me."

"I... I." Hope couldn't say the words.

Her *mamm* began to smile. It was a beautiful sight that lit up her face. "Are you courting? Is that what it is?"

Hope swallowed and nodded. Maybe this wouldn't be so hard. "I think I might be."

"That is wonderful news. Who is it?" Anna asked, her face lit up with joy.

Hope froze, for she knew her *mamm* would not be happy. But maybe they could talk this through, and her *mamm* would give Andy a chance... she opened her mouth to speak when Karen came over from the counter.

"There is trouble in the back, Anna. Samuel is out, and we need you."

Anna smiled at her and then at Hope. "I'm so happy and proud of you. We will talk later." With that, she got up, kissed Hope on the cheek, and almost ran into the back of the bakery.

"Sorry," Karen said before she walked away, looking sheepish.

Once she was alone at the table, Hope felt tears pushing at the back of her eyes. They wanted to escape and run down her face, but she wouldn't let them. Along with the tears was a sense of desolation and loneliness. It was always the same. The bakery was always more important. She would go to Andy and tell him, *jah*. Maybe if her *mamm* had spoken to her, it would have changed her mind, but not now, *nee*, she was doing this.

CHAPTER THREE

* * *

The LORD is my strength and my defense ;
he has become my salvation
Psalm 118:14

* * *

As he walked up to the bishop's *haus*, Andy felt his palms begin to sweat. What was he going to say? He stopped and rubbed his hands on his thick black work trousers and took a breath. Maybe this was the wrong thing to do. Maybe he should just keep his head down and forget Hope? Maybe this was a mistake, and he should just go home. As he started to turn, a voice stopped him.

"Andy, I could do with a rest. Would you like a *kaffe*?"

Andy looked up to see Bishop Amos Beiler standing from behind a bush in his garden. Amos took off his hat, wiped his brow, rubbed a hand through his gray hair, and then tugged on his long gray beard.

"*Jah, denke...* if it is not too much trouble," Andy said, but his words were little more than a squeak.

"It is *nee* trouble at all. Come on in." There was a big smile on the bishop's wrinkled face and a welcome in his faded blue eyes. For a moment, Andy felt better. The bishop would not judge him in the way that others had... would he?

"It is *gut* to see you," Sarah, the bishop's *fraa* said as Amos took Andy through the kitchen to the dining room.

"You too, Sarah," Andy managed, feeling so small and unworthy.

Soon, they were sitting around the old wooden table and drinking strong *kaffe* with a slice of strawberry cake each. Andy understood that Amos would wait for him to relax, but he was not sure that he could. His stomach was turning, and he was sweating.

Amos simply smiled and munched on the cake. His long gray beard, the symbol of marriage, moved as he ate. Would Andy ever have the right to grow a beard? He hoped so and took a sip of *kaffe* and then managed a bite of cake. What was he going to say?

"Relax," Amos said. "You are amongst friends here."

"*Denke.* I know I am disliked, but do you think I could ever court?"

"We will return to your likability later, but, of course, you can court; why shouldn't you?" Amos asked.

"The trouble... it followed me back from my *rumspringa.* *Nee* one trusts me." Andy swallowed. Why was Amos being so nice to him?

"I do not think they know you, and maybe it is time for you to let them see the real you. Perhaps, you could tell me what happened on your *rumspringa?*"

A smile crossed Andy's face. This was what he had always wanted. For the district to know the truth. Now he had his chance to talk... so, why was he holding back?

The problem was that to clear his own name, he had to blacken that of another. It was someone, who, in his opinion, deserved it, but even so, it was not something that he could do. Yet doing so would free him to court, so, why was he holding back?

"Talk to me," Amos said.

"I cannot say much, but I did not beat that man. I promise you that. I was trying to help him when the police arrived." Andy knew that he sounded like a *kinner* making excuses, and he knew that Amos would not believe him. After all, he had *nee* proof.

"I believe you, and I know there is much more to this story. Do you feel able to tell it to me?"

Andy shook his head. "Not just yet."

"Then tell me what you can," Amos said, his eyes offering comfort and support, his head bowed a little as he leaned forward, eager to hear the truth.

A sigh escaped Andy. It was so clear that Amos believed him, that he had faith in him, and such understanding almost brought tears to his eyes. *Should he tell him everything?*

Amos took another bite of his cake, giving Andy time to think. Many would believe him if he told the whole truth, and he would be exonerated... or would he? Many would say that he was just lying to save his bacon! That if it was true, why had he left it so long? There was no winning this war of words. He had left it too long. If he blackened another's name now, he would be poorly judged, and rightly so.

Taking a bite of his own cake, he swallowed and then sipped at the *kaffe*. It was getting cold; had he really been here that long? It had seemed like mere minutes since he walked in, but in that time, much had changed. But was that change for the better or for the worse?

It was time to talk. "As I said, I did not beat that man. Unfortunately, or maybe, fortunately... I arrived to find another attacking him." Andy was taken back to the night in question, he shuddered. The attack had been ruthless and brutal, and there had been a look of insanity in the attacker's eyes. "I intervened. I pulled him off, and I got punched in the process." It had taken some time to stop the attack, and he was covered in blood during the scuffle. He ended up with a black eye and a cut lip, and one of his fists was damaged when he struck the man to stop him from attacking. Andy paused, he was on the verge of naming the man who deserved punishment for this, but that was not their way. If he did that, was it for selfish reasons?

"I can see that you are torn. I understand," Amos said. "You can tell me in confidence if you wish."

Andy swallowed and looked down at his hands. They were calloused and weather-worn, but that was not what he saw. In his mind, they were soaked in blood, and he felt guilt. He had known that the attack would take place, and yet he had walked away and let it. He had not wanted to get involved. That was his shame; a man was left disabled because he walked away.

"*Nee*, I cannot say anything yet, for I am to blame. I knew it was going to happen, and I walked away. If I had stayed, maybe I could have stopped it all."

"Then leave out the names, if you must, but tell me everything," Amos said, and this time his voice was stern and commanding.

Andy felt his mouth open, and the words streamed out. All his life, he had done what the bishop said, and he could not stop himself from doing so now.

"They were arguing over a woman called Candy." Andy felt his ears warming as heat flushed his face. "Steven, the man who was hurt, laughed at...." He could not say the name. "Then Steven walked out. My friend... acquaintance, was drunk... I was not... I had had a drink but not much." He lowered his head; he had just admitted to drinking, he was only making this worse.

"It is all right." Amos reached across and touched Andy's hand. "We understand *rumspringa*. If we judged everyone who had a drink, there would not be many left."

"My acquaintance, let's call him Mr. A, got angry and left the bar. I followed him to see Steven leaning against his car with Candy. Mr. A was so angry, his fury was like a force, and he screamed abuse." He paused momentarily, reliving the event, feeling the cold breeze on his skin, his heart racing, and knowing he should stop it from happening. "I grabbed ahold of him. I told him to walk away, but he pulled free and flew across the parking lot." Andy dropped his head and looked down at his hands. The skin on his nails was dry and cracking.

"Go on," Amos said.

"A fight began, and Candy ran past me and back into the bar. I didn't want to get involved, so I ran in myself and told them to call the police. I sat down, but after a few minutes, I felt guilty, so I went outside. It was awful. Steven was on the ground, being brutally kicked and punched. I pulled Mr. A off, and we fought. Then he ran away, and I dropped to my knees to help Steven. That was when the police arrived." Andy felt a huge sense of relief to have told the truth, and he looked up. Would Amos believe him?

CHAPTER FOUR

* * *

4 One thing I ask of the LORD, this is what I seek:
that I may dwell in the house of the LORD all the days of
my life,
to gaze upon the beauty of the LORD and to seek him in
his temple.
Psalm 27:4

* * *

H ope fought back the tears as she watched her *mamm* disappear. Should she go home, should she go and see Andy, or should she sit here and wait for her *mamm* to return? It could take

26

forever. Once Anna got in the kitchen, the world shrank; that was all she saw.

Hope took another bite of the delicious and moist cookie, but for some reason, it felt like ash in her throat, and she wondered if she would start to cough. Oh, she had to just say this, or she would end up courting who they wanted. Andy meant so much to her; it was the right decision... wasn't it?

Suddenly, she was filled with fire and anger, and despair. It was as if all her emotions were pouring out of her in one go, and it was unbearable. She had to talk to her *mamm* now... but the kitchen was... it was not a part of her life, and she always felt like an intruder there.

"Would you like more *kaffe*?"

Hope looked up to see Karen smiling down at her. At just sixteen, the redhead was three years younger than Hope, yet she always made Hope feel young. There was something serious and adult about Karen's deep green eyes and serious face.

"*Denke.*" Hope looked away, feeling guilty for intruding on this space, for disturbing her *mamm*. *Nee*, she had every right to be here and felt anger rising inside her once more. It grew and spread like wildfire, consuming her guilt and her doubt. "Will my *mamm* be free soon?"

"*Jah*, it was just a customer... one that is hard to handle," Karen said with a smile. "Why don't you go back and see her?"

"*Denke*, I will...." Karen was staring at her, expecting her to move. "I will just finish this delicious cookie first."

Karen gave a weak smile and wandered to the next table with her *kaffe* pot. Hope breathed a sigh of relief, and she nibbled on the cookie. This time it tasted delicious. It filled her with sugar and boosted her confidence. She could do this.

Once she had finished her food and drank the *kaffe*, Hope knew that her time had come. If she was to do this, then she needed to do it now before her anger dissipated.

Standing, she wandered over to the counter. There was still a queue, and for a moment, she nearly smiled and walked out. The problem was, if she did, she would never get the chance to talk to her *mamm*. It was not that Anna was a bad *mamm*; she was not. In fact, she had been brilliant... it was just that she loved her work and got so involved. Hope knew that Anna would talk to her if she let her know how much she wanted to talk. She also knew that she was doing this out of a touch of rebellion. Though she never believed that Andy had hurt a man, he couldn't do it, and she didn't know what had happened. So, why hadn't she forced him to tell her?

Karen looked strangely at her, so Hope ducked under the counter with a smile, pushed through the door, and walked into the kitchen.

Her *mamm* was standing at one of the stainless steel tables adding ingredients to a big bowl. There was a smile on her face that made Hope hesitate. She knew her *mamm* would not approve.

"Hope, come on over," Anna said, waving her across. "Sorry, we are busy today, but I can stop if you need something."

"*Nee, Mamm*, I just wanted to tell you something."

Anna stopped and rubbed the flour off her hands. She clasped them together and smiled. "*Jah*, who is it that you are courting?"

Hope hesitated. She hadn't even said *jah* to him yet; maybe she should wait.

"It is okay. I know you, and I will support you in anything," Anna said.

"Andy Byler invited me to service, and I said *jah*," the words burst out of her in a long stream. She watched her *mamm's* expression go from joy at the thought of her courting to horror at her choice of man.

"What, who?" Anna's eyes were open wide, and her mouth had dropped open.

"My *gut* friend, Andy Byler. You remember we spent so much time together as *kinner*."

"*Nee*, I won't allow it." Anna was shaking her head

The world had stopped, and Andy held his breath. Then, slowly, a smile spread across the bishop's face. "I believe you," Amos said. "I'm so pleased that you have finally told me this."

"I can't mention names," Andy managed through the lump of gratitude and joy lodged in his throat. It didn't matter if nothing else came of this; Amos believed him, and that was enough.

"You don't need to. I know who was away, and I know people. That is something that I have to deal with, but for now, we need to change the way people see you. It might take time, but it will happen."

"I asked Hope to service. I know it can never happen...." Andy stopped as his ears burned and his cheeks flushed with heat.

"I have seen you two as friends all your life. I suspected that more would come of it." Amos smiled. "I never expected you to go on *rumspringa*, and I understand why you did. The death of your parents was a tragedy. You overcame it well and should be proud. Hope is a strong woman. If she likes you, in that way, she will make her own mind up over what happened. Just relax and know that this was a test, and you returned a stronger and better man for it."

Andy smiled. It felt *gut* to have the bishop on his side and believing in him, but there was *nee* practical help. How was he to get Hope's parents to accept him?

Amos chuckled. "I can see you are impatient. But, trust in me and trust in *Gott*; all will be well."

CHAPTER FIVE

* * *

See, I am doing a new thing!
Now it springs up; do you not perceive it?
I am making a way in the desert and streams in the
wasteland.
Isaiah 43:19

* * *

H ope turned and ran, this time she went out
of the bakery's back door and almost ran
into her *daed.* Samuel stepped to one side as
Hope barged past. "What is it?" he called after her.

Hope hesitated, she could always talk to her *daed,* but she could hear Anna calling, and the last thing she wanted was another lecture from her *mamm.* Shaking her head and wiping away her tears, she picked up her skirts and ran.

Anna came out the back door to see Samuel looking confused. "Where's Hope?" she asked.

"She just ran away. Is everything all right?" There was worry in Samuel's brown eyes

"*Ack,* I think I said the wrong thing," Anna said. "I should go after her."

"*Nee,* let her have some space. You can talk to her later." Samuel reached down and kissed his *fraa's* cheek. "You know our *dochder.* She is strong, and she will be fine."

"I guess," Anna said, but there was a deep worry inside her. How come she always seemed to say the wrong thing? However, she did not want Hope to court Andy Byler. The whole district knew about his fight. Andy had disabled a man. Such violence terrified her. That was not the sort of man she wanted Hope mixed up with.

"Come, let's have a *kaffe,* and you can tell me what happened," Samuel said as he led her into the bakery.

Anna relaxed. Samuel was so calm and solid, her rock, and he would know how to resolve this.

Hope almost knocked her *daed* over as she fled the bakery. She wanted to stop and talk to him but could hear her *mamm*'s shouting getting closer. There was anger in her voice, and she did not wish to face it. Instead, she ran faster down the lane and through a gate into a field. As she ran, her tears fell, and she wondered if it was anger or worry she had heard in her *mamm's* voice. It didn't matter, Andy was her friend, and her *mamm* had been wrong to discount him without listening. Why would *nee* one give him a chance?

She ran across the field, ignoring the confused looks on the faces of the cattle as she streamed past them. Her *kapp* almost came off, and she grabbed onto it and at last slowed down. That was when she realized that she was close to the farm where Andy worked and lived.

Should she go home, or should she talk to him?

"Hope, it is *gut* to see you," Andy called from her left.

Hope turned to see him walking down the lane to the farm. He must wonder why she was running across the fields, but he said nothing, simply smiling at her as he made his way over.

"It is *gut* to see you too," she said. There was something different in his eyes, in his stance. He looked stronger, more sure of himself than she had seen in a long time.

"Come, I have *kaffe* and some cherry pie if you are hungry?"

"*Denke*, but the *kaffe* will do fine," she said, for the cookies she had eaten were feeling a little heavy after her mad dash across the fields.

"Where have you been?" she asked, then her mouth dropped open. That had sounded rude and demanding.

He chuckled. "I just went to see Bishop Amos."

"That is *gut*," she said, and then her heart missed a beat, was he in trouble?

"Do not worry, I just wanted some advice... and as always, he made me feel so much better."

Hope chuckled back. "Then that is why you have a spring in your step."

"It is indeed." They had walked back to the *farmhaus*, and he opened the door and held it for her to walk in.

"*Gut* day, Hope, Andy," Kanagy said. "It is *gut* to see you, but I have some paperwork to attend to. So if you don't mind, I will leave you two to talk."

"*Denke*, it is *gut* to see you too," Hope said, watching him leave the room. There was a little bend in his shoulders, and he was looking a little thin, but there was still strength in him.

She knew her way around the kitchen, and before Andy had even removed his hat and boots, she had the stove door open and was adding more wood. Andy filled the kettle, and together they made *kaffe*.

Soon, they were sitting at the table, both clinging to their mugs and feeling sheepish. The question of him inviting her to service hung between them. Hope wanted to say *jah*, but she was nervous. She wanted to talk to him about her *mamm's* reaction, but she feared that it would hurt him.

Finally, he coughed and took her hand. "I understand," he said.

Hope looked up at him, and she saw defeat in his eyes. It cut her to the bone, and she knew she could not bear to hurt him. It hit her there and then that she wanted to court him, as she always had.

"What?" she said.

Andy chuckled. "I understand that my reputation has come between us. You do not have to worry about not wanting to court me. Maybe, one day I will be seen as suitable again, but do not worry, for Amos is supporting me, so I will be fine."

Hope smiled. "You don't understand." She winked at him. "I can see that you still talk too much and too fast when you are nervous. I came here to say *jah*. *Jah*, I would love you to drive me to service this Sunday. I will be proud to be seen with you." She folded her arms and sat up a little straighter. The look of shock that crossed his face was amusing, but the hope she saw there filled her with joy.

"That is fantastic news," Kanagy said from the other room. "Why don't you take Hope for a ride in the buggy?"

CHAPTER SIX

30 The fruit of the righteous is a tree of life,
and the one who is wise saves lives.
31 If the righteous receive their due on earth,
how much more the ungodly and the sinner!
Proverbs 11:30-31

Marlin Kanagy sipped on his *kaffe* as he watched the buggy corner too fast as it turned onto his farm. He pulled on his beard and sighed. *What now!*

The horse was hauled to a halt not moments later, sweat ran down its flanks, and it was panting heavily. The sun reflected off the buggy, and the driver was hidden. However, it seemed like it was time for Bishop Amos to visit the Glick farm once more.

For a moment, Marlin's mind retreated back in time. The smiling face of his *fraa*, Sylvia, was there before him. Even to this day, he still remembered her as a young woman. Beautiful, full of life and fire. Once, she had stopped another Glick from raising his whip to his horse and pushing it too far. That had been Jacob, and even though he had not yet seen inside the buggy, Marlin knew that it was Simon Glick driving it.

Remembering that incident filled him with rage. Jacob had turned his whip on Sylvia. Luckily, Bishop Amos had been there and had pulled it from his hands before it could fall. Those who witnessed the event said they thought, for one moment, that Amos Beiler, their bishop, would turn the whip on Jacob. But, of course, he didn't, and *nee* one heard what he said to Jacob, but the man's face turned white, and he changed from that day forward.

The change lasted for some time, but Jacob was an arrogant man, entitled by his wealth, and his son followed in his footsteps. *Nee* one else in the district behaved like the Glicks. They were egotistical, entitled, rude and aggressive. Usually, they kept it below the line where the bishop would be involved, but not always.

How Jacob ever got the sweet Mary Swann to marry him, Marlin would never know. But, unfortunately, the boy didn't seem to have gained much from his *gut mamm*.

The door to the buggy opened, and Simon climbed down. He stretched his back and turned away, looking slowly around the farm before he turned back, eventually acknowledging Marlin.

Marlin hid his smile; this was all an act. The boy was posturing, but why? He had nothing to gain here. There was nothing that Marlin could do for him.

Marlin took another sip of *kaffe* and leaned back in his chair. For a moment, he thought about pulling his hat over his eyes and feigning sleep. But that would not do. That would be rude.

"*Gut* day, Old Man Kanagy," Simon said as he strutted up to the chair where Marlin rested. "I would love to share some *kaffe* with you while we discuss the farm."

Simon glanced around for a chair. The only other one nearby was piled high with clothes needing mending. Lydia Bender was coming for those later. Marlin could see the indecision in the young man; he wanted to sit but was unsure what to do. "It's Marlin or Mr. Kanagy to you," Marlin said. "Only my friends get to call me Old Man Kanagy. Now, what do you want?" The bite in his voice was clear; so much for not being rude! It didn't matter. He could not be nice to the cocky young ginger-headed man who was the spitting image of the man who nearly beat his Sylvia.

Simon laughed a little too loud, and then the smile slipped off his face as he saw that Marlin was not laughing. He looked away as if looking for support or for escape, but taking a breath, he turned back. "I came to buy your farm."

Marlin felt like a hand had reached into his chest and stopped his heart with cold icy fingers. There was something in the way that Simon said this that made him feel threatened. It was not the words or even the tone. It was the strangest thing, a surety that the farm would be his. "The farm is not for sale." Swallowing, he leaned back, ensuring he looked relaxed and confident.

"Everything is for sale," Simon said. "I have the money. You have no relatives; why not enjoy the money while you... still can?"

"I have everything I need to enjoy my life," Marlin said.

Simon's cheeks turned red, and he clenched his fists, scrunching up the rim of his hat. "Don't be a foolish old man. All this work for what?"

"Because it is my farm, and it is up to me who I leave it to. Now, I think it's time you left. Your horse could do with some water."

"You have water. He can drink here." Simon walked back to his horse, swaggering a little despite his defeat. He pulled on the reins to drag the animal to a trough.

"*Nee.*" Marlin was on his feet and stood between the trough and the horse. "The way you drive him, he will colic if he fills himself with water. Go now, and drive home at a decent pace, or I will speak to Amos."

Rage filled Simon's eyes, and fear curdled in Marlin's stomach. It didn't matter. He stood his ground. The young man tried to force him to move, but Kanagy was not moving. This was his farm, and he would never let it go. The only way a Glick would get it would be over his dead body.

Simon let out a breath, sounding like a child having a tantrum. He turned, muttering, and jumped back into his buggy. He hauled the horse around and left the property at a fast trot.

Marlin let out a breath of relief. That could have gone much worse. He watched the horse traverse the lane. It was going at a brisk pace but not a punishing one. There was nothing to report here. A strange feeling of foreboding settled in his gut; he wished there had been. Something told him he hadn't heard the last of this.

"You look very happy this morning," Marlin said as he entered the kitchen Sunday morning. "Service does not usually fill you with such joy."

Andy felt heat hit his ears, and his cheeks were burning. "I... I guess I am." Andy turned away from the eggs he was frying and smiled.

"I'm teasing you, lad. I know why you're so happy. It will be a fine day for courting." Marlin eased into a chair and pulled himself to the table. A *kaffe* was already waiting for him, and he supped it with a smile.

"I just hope that things... well, that people don't cause trouble," Andy said as he pulled the warmed bread from another pan and put it on two plates. Then he slid the bacon on top of them and carried the plates to the table.

"*Ack*, don't let foolish people's opinions bother you. You are right for that girl. I can see the way you look at each other."

"*Denke*. I just hope others will see it that way. My hopes are up for Hope." He shrugged at his joke and sat down.

"You always make this so nice. The bacon fat you fry the bread with... it's delicious," Kanagy said.

Andy understood the old man was changing the subject. If he thought too much about it, he would panic. What if he said the wrong thing? What if he made a fool of himself? What if people told Hope to get away from him? *Nee*, it was best if he was distracted. "Whose buggy did I see driving away yesterday?"

"Well, that was a strange conversation if ever I had one." Kanagy shook his head. His beard and hair shook with him. "It was Simon Glick. He wanted to buy the farm. Can you believe that?"

Andy felt his blood freeze. Was he about to lose his job and his home?

"Don't look so worried, lad. I'm not leaving this place until they carry me out, and for that, I need you." He waved his left hand, holding the fork. "So, don't you go getting married and moving away."

Andy froze once more. He hadn't really thought about marriage. Well, he had but not in practical terms. Not in terms of where they would live. Of course, this made him realize he wanted to marry Hope and live here with her. Marlin Kanagy was like a *daed* to him, and he would never let the old man down.

"Smile and eat," Kanagy said. "And don't worry about Simon. He understood I don't wish to sell."

Andy did smile, and he pushed Simon from his mind. One thing he knew was that Kanagy could handle the arrogant young man. What he had to worry about was if Hope's parents would let him drive her to service and what sort of reception he would get once they got there." The bacon grease suddenly felt heavy in his stomach.

CHAPTER SEVEN

* * *

What, then, shall we say in response to these things?
If God is for us, who can be against us?
Romans 8:3 1

* * *

"I will not allow this," Anna said, her cheeks flushed with anger, her hands clasped in her apron, screwing the pristine white cloth into a ball.

"But, *Mamm*, why?" Hope asked. She was trying desperately to hold on to her anger. To stop it from getting free and forcing something she would regret to pop out of her mouth before she could stop it.

"Because of who he is," Anna said, her voice rising with her own anger. "Because you could be in danger."

"*Mamm*, don't be silly. I spent as much time with Andy as I did with you when I was growing up. You know him. You know he wouldn't do what they said he did." Hope felt as if she was losing, and the more her *mamm* pushed her, the more she was determined to stick by Andy. "This is so unfair." She almost stamped her foot for a moment, just as she had when she was a *kinner*.

Anna laughed. "It is a long time since I've seen that attitude. I'm trying to keep you safe." Anna turned to her husband across the table. "Samuel, what do you think?"

Samuel sipped on his *kaffe* and then sucked on his teeth. Taking his time as he often did. Then he turned to Hope. "I understand what you are saying. Before he went on his *rumspringa*, I would have been delighted if you had courted Andy. His parents were *gut* people. You two grew up together, and he was always a *gut* person whenever I met him. Now, I'm not so sure...."

Hope sighed, and Anna nodded in agreement, letting go of the apron she clutched onto the back of a chair.

"Hold on," Samuel said. "I could never get my head around what happened. The boy who left here would not have done such a thing. I believe he is hiding what really happened."

"That is as bad as committing the crime," Anna said and took a seat at the table next to Hope and opposite Samuel.

"Is it?" Samuel asked. "If he is protecting another, then it is our way." He looked at Anna for long moments, and Hope could see something passing between them. It was understanding and trust, and she hoped she could one day appreciate and love someone this much.

At last, Samuel turned to her. "*Dochder*, we both love you very much. We will allow you to court Andy...."

Hope let out a whoop of joy.

Samuel held up one finger. "But, you will not go anywhere alone, and you will stop this if we ask you to. Is that clear?"

Hope was struggling to keep a huge grin off her face. She nodded and felt full of joy. There would be *nee* circumstances when they would ask her to stop. "*Denke*." She rushed around the table and kissed her *daed* on the cheek and then her *mamm*.

"Go, see to the chickens before he gets here," Samuel said.

Hope left the room feeling like she could float across the yard to the chicken pen. They didn't have many hens, just a dozen, but it helped with the bakery, and she found them relaxing. Only this morning, she would not be lingering in the pen; she couldn't wait for Andy to arrive.

"Do you think this is safe?" Anna asked.

"Hope is right; we know this boy, this man. Do you really see him as a vicious brute?"

"I don't... but I'm not so sure that I would risk Hope's life."

Andy's hands were slick with sweat as he trotted the buggy toward the Miller's *haus*. What would he do if they would not allow Anna to come with him? But, of course, there was nothing he could do. He would just have to accept it and pray that, in time, he could rehabilitate his reputation.

He turned into the yard attached to the *haus*. The *haus* was behind the bakery on one side and in front of it on another. As he did, he noticed an *Englischer* car driving past and turning toward Kanagy's farm. Who was it, and what did they want? The thought of Simon Glick buying the farm reared its ugly head in his mind. Was this something to do with that?

The vehicle drove past Kanagy's, and he sighed in relief. That was when he noticed that Anna and Samuel Miller were standing in front of him and staring. Oh dear, here it came!

They looked annoyed.

"You need to concentrate if you are to drive our *dochder*," Samuel said.

Andy let out a sigh and climbed out. "I apologize. I was just watching to see if the *Englischer* was going to Kanagy's. I meant *nee* disrespect." He patted the horse on the neck as he walked around to them. "*Gut* morning." He took off his hat and held it in front of him. "I would like your permission to drive Hope to service."

"You have it... for now," Samuel said.

Andy wanted to run into Samuel's arms. He had spent so much time with them when he was growing up. Then there had been two years when he didn't see them so much. First, his *daed* died, and then his *mamm* was ill. After that, he couldn't cope and ran away on his *rumspringa*. How he regretted that decision now. It was made under the pain of grief and doubt and had destroyed his life. These *gut* people would have helped him. But at the time, it hurt so much that he needed to escape.

"Andy, *gut* morning," Hope called, and he spun around to see her walking toward him. The sun was behind her and seemed to make her glow with joy. A huge smile was spread across her pretty face, and the sunlight reflected off her freckles.

"*Gut* morning, are you ready?" he blurted out.

Hope handed a bucket with eggs to her *mamm*, kissed her parents' cheeks, and nodded. Andy took her hand and helped her into the buggy. That touch filled him with joy; he knew he was blushing. "*Gut* day. I will take *gut* care of her and see you at service," he said, touching his hat before climbing into the buggy and setting the horse to walk out of the drive.

So far, this had gone better than he could have hoped, so why did he feel so worried?

CHAPTER EIGHT

* * *

2 Many are saying of me, "God will not deliver him."
3 But you, LORD, are a shield around me, my glory,
the One who lifts my head high.
4 I call out to the LORD,
and he answers me from his holy mountain.
5 I lie down and sleep;
I wake again, because the LORD sustains me.
6 I will not fear though tens of thousands assail me on
every side.
Psalm 3:2-6

* * *

"How are you?" Andy asked as the horse trotted along the lane. "I'm so pleased that you agreed to come with me."

"Of course, I agreed," Hope said. "We have always been such friends." She watched as his cheeks flushed red, and he took a breath. Although she almost giggled, he thought she was saying this was just friendship. "I didn't mean it like that. I wanted to come with you. I believe in you, and I want to see... well... I look forward to our courting."

"Me too." He turned and smiled.

Hope felt her heart flutter. When had things changed between them? She didn't remember it happening. One day they were friends, and the next, she noticed how strong his arms were. How handsome his smile was and how his eyes sparkled when he laughed. She had fallen for him, and she had fallen hard. What would she do if people were awful to them, to her?

"Don't look so worried. I will take *gut* care of you, and Bouncer here is a strong and reliable horse."

"I'm not worried." Though she said the words, she realized that she was worrying her bottom lip, a sure sign that she was worried.

He chuckled. "I know you well. Bishop Amos believes in me. I promise you that bit by bit, the rest of the district will do too."

"I know they will," she said.

Soon they arrived at the service. It was at the Schrock barn, and many buggies were already there. Andy pulled in behind the buggy of Mary, Rueben, & Lucy Wagler. The Schrock brothers ran a dairy, and this was their place. James Schrock helped Reuban unharness his horse. Mary and Lucy climbed down while Hope and Andy waited.

Lucy's eyes widened with delight, and she ran over. Mary's eyes widened with some other emotion that Hope did not wish to dwell on.

"I am so excited for you," Lucy said, opening the buggy door.

"Wait, just a moment," Andy said, and he jumped down and ran around to help her down.

Hope knew that she was blushing as she took his hand. Lucy was grinning in delight for her. Hope felt the butterflies take flight in her stomach at the touch of Andy's hand as he helped her down.

"Go talk," he said. "I will catch up with you once Bouncer is sorted.

Hope smiled, but she could see over Andy's shoulder that Jonas Schrock looked angry. *Why was that?*

"What are you doing with Hope?" Jonas asked Andy.

"We are courting," Andy said and led his horse forward. Traditionally, Jonas would help him unharness the animal and show him where to put him. Only Jonas looked like his cream had curdled and smelt really bad. He walked past Andy to the next buggy that was pulling in.

Andy seemed to stoop under the pressure momentarily, but he turned and smiled at her. Then he raised his head, stroked Bouncer, and undid the harness. He rose above the petty treatment, and Hope was proud of him.

"Come, I fancy a lemonade before the service," Lucy said, taking Hope by the arm. "Also, you have a lot to tell me."

Hope and Lucy grabbed a glass of lemonade and walked over to a bench. They had arrived early for the service and would have time to talk.

"I never believed your parents would let you court Andy!" Lucy said.

"They have known him all his life. So they know the rumors are not true."

"Oh, I don't know... the police brought him back, and he was so beaten up and bruised," Lucy said, and then her eyes widened. "I'm sorry. I know how *gut* friends you two were, but... be careful."

"I... I can't explain it. I know he didn't do those things."

"That is what you hope, Hope." Lucy began to giggle, but her expression changed under Hope's worried gaze. "*Nee*, if you believe in him, then I do too. He was never aggressive or in trouble at school. Always kind and the one that stopped trouble. I believe you."

"See, I've already doubled the number of people who believe in him, and Bishop Amos does, so what could go wrong?"

The look on Jonas Schrock's face was like a slap across Andy's cheek. It stung. Clearly, the older man was not happy that he had driven Hope to service. Andy had not even unharnessed his horse, and he was already feeling the hatred. It hurt, and he knew that Hope would see it. Fatigue hung heavy on him until he remembered the smile that Sarah and Amos Beiler had given him. They were not false or forced but were genuinely happy to see him. He would trust the bishop, and he would get through this. He smiled at Hope and raised his head. After all, he had every right to be here and to court her.

It didn't take long to unharness Bouncer and turn him in the paddock with the other geldings. The horse trotted over to a friend, and the two pranced around the paddock for a moment. It was a *gut* sight; at least his horse had friends.

Turning away, he began to maneuver his buggy when James Schrock slapped a hand on his shoulder. "Let me help you."

"*Denke*," he said. Together, they pushed the buggy to the side with all the others. Raising the shafts and tipping it up so that it took up less room. It was not a difficult job and was one he did all the time at home; it was just the principle of doing it alone here. It made him look different; it ostracized him. The district stuck together, they helped each other, and this tiny act of kindness meant the world to Andy.

"Don't worry about my brother," James said, "Jonas can be cantankerous at times." He winked before turning to help the next family.

Andy wondered when Kanagy would arrive, a neighbor was fetching him, and for some reason, he felt worried. Was it because of the visit from the Glick boy, the vehicle he had seen heading that way, or maybe it was just the change that was happening. Life would never be the same if he continued courting Hope. That thought shocked him. He wanted this, so why was he second-guessing his decision. Then he looked up and saw a circle of angry faces staring at him. That was why.

CHAPTER NINE

* * *

So then, brothers and sisters,
stand firm and hold fast to the teachings we passed on
to you,
whether by word of mouth or by letter.
2 Thessalonians 2:15

* * *

Andy could see Hope talking to Lucy, and he didn't know what to do. He seemed to be rocking on the spot as he thought about going this way or that but was moving *neewhere.*

"Hope could do so much better," a voice said behind him.

"He should never have been allowed back," another said to his left.

Everywhere he turned, people were whispering and staring, and he felt as if the world was going black. Maybe he should leave?

"Andy, this way, please," a commanding voice called.

Andy looked up to see Bishop Amos Beiler walking toward him with a big smile on his face. "I'm so pleased you could help me today," Amos said, beckoning for Andy to follow him.

"Of course, Amos. Anything you ever need."

"This is the sort of man we need in this district," Amos said. "We are so lucky to have men like you." The bishop's voice had been loud, it carried, and the stares melted away as his words and sentiment spread through the crowd.

At first, Andy felt uncomfortable at the service. Next to him on the benches was Kanagy. The old man reached out and touched his hand and gave him a reassuring smile. It helped. Kanagy had never judged him, had never asked him what happened, and treated him the same as he had before Andy left. If only more could do so.

Amos, as always, gave an uplifting and inspiring sermon. Today, he spoke about sin and about redemption. He reminded them that only he who is without sin, could throw the first stone. And he knew that a few would be feeling uncomfortable at these words. But he also knew they would help his reputation, but how much? Would it be enough for people to allow him to court Hope?

As the service finished, everyone drifted outside, where benches were set up in the spring sunshine. "Go see your girl," Kanagy said.

"Let me get you seated first and something to eat."

Kanagy stood up and chuckled. "I'm not that old. I will join you at the table. Go now. I know how exciting this can be."

Andy gave his friend and mentor a grin of appreciation. But did he notice a touch of sorrow in Kanagy's blue eyes? Was he remembering his own *fraa*?

Outside, the tables and benches were all set up and already loaded with food. The air was fresh, the sun shining, and birds sang in the trees behind them. It was idyllic. People were talking and laughing. For a moment, he felt like he was back before his *rumspringa*. It felt *gut*.

Like many women, Hope was helping carry out the meal. Lucy was working with her, and the two of them chatted and giggled as they went back and forward. Looking at her filled Andy's heart with joy, but then he glanced across at her parents and saw the two of them, heads bowed and talking. They looked worried. He hated that he was causing such worry and wanted them to accept him like they had when he was a *kinner*. But would it ever be possible?

Hope noticed that Andy was standing and staring, and he looked so lost. Taking a more circular route with the last dish, she came up next to him. "Come and sit with my family and me," she said.

"I worry that I am putting strain on your family," he said, glancing over at the table. Anna looked so worried.

The sadness in his eyes almost broke Hope's heart. "After the rain, there was sunshine," she said, giving him her most radiant smile. It worked. He looked a little better. "I know you didn't do that awful thing, and soon, my parents will know too. Trust the bishop and come and join me." It was clear that her words had lifted some of the burden from his shoulders, but he still looked a little broken. It didn't matter; she trusted and believed in him and would see his reputation redeemed.

Hope sat beside her parents, with Anna on her left and Samuel beside him. There was an empty place across the table next to Marlin Kanagy. Hope smiled. It looked like Andy's mentor was looking out for him too. Kanagy winked at her as she took her seat, and she gave him a smile of appreciation.

For a moment, the conversation stopped, and *nee* one was reaching for food. Hope felt a touch of worry whirl in her stomach. She needed to break the silence. "Wasn't that an inspiring sermon today?"

For a moment, she thought that Mary, who was sitting across the table, looked a little annoyed. But luckily, Lucy understood.

"Bishop Amos always knows exactly what to say," Lucy said. "I know I had judged others when I had no right to do so. Don't you agree, *Mamm*?"

It looked as if Mary would disagree for a moment, but then she reached out for some fried chicken. "It was certainly an interesting sermon."

That did it, the conversation began to spread around the table, and everyone was reaching for food and chatting naturally. Though Andy was keeping out of it a little, she noticed a slight smile had spread across his face. Slowly, they would do this, and she was happy to take the time. She knew that he was worth it.

After the meal was over, everyone was starting to drift away, and Andy felt his nerves kick in once more. Luckily, the meal had not gone too badly due to Hope, Lucy, and Kanagy's influence. No one had insulted him, and no one had said anything about him courting Hope. Perhaps, they were avoiding it rather than accepting it, but it was better than an outright attack.

Swallowing, he said his goodbyes to Kanagy and walked across to Anna, Samuel, and Hope. "I really enjoyed today," he said. "I would like permission to drive your *dochder* home." Why had he said that? He didn't need to ask permission, for he already had it by driving her here.

However, he noticed that Samuel seemed pleased with the question.

Before Anna could open her mouth to say *nee*, Samuel touched her arm. "You have it. As you have the support of Bishop Amos, then you have mine."

"*Denke*," he said.

Hope turned and kissed her *mamm* and *daed* on the cheek before waving at Lucy and noting for him to lead the way.

His heart soared, for he could see the joy in her eyes, but before he turned away, he saw the anger and fear on Anna's face. He had a long way to go before he was accepted. He just hoped that nothing could go wrong, that he could rehabilitate his reputation and marry this wonderful woman — one day.

CHAPTER TEN

* * *

I will give them an undivided heart and put a new spirit in them;
I will remove from them their heart of stone and give them a heart of flesh.
Ezekiel 11:19

* * *

The drive home was wonderful. Hope was chattering away busily like she always had done in the past. That was one thing about her he loved. She rarely stopped speaking. She was so filled with enthusiasm. She was both Hope by name and hope by nature, and he loved her for it.

"You were really starting to win people over. I am so pleased that Bishop Amos has taken you under his wing."

Hope bumped his arm with hers as she finished speaking, and he looked down to see the radiant smile on her pretty face. For a moment, he wanted to reach across and stroke the line of freckles across her cheek. But he took in a breath. That was way to forward. *What was he thinking?*

Hope chuckled. "Don't look so serious. This may take time, but we have time, and we will do it. People will soon see the real you, as I do!"

"Your belief in me is enough," he said, blinking, for suddenly, his eyes must have been affected by dust from the road, for they were full of tears.

"It's not enough for me." She chuckled. "Wasn't Lucy wonderful?"

"*Jah*, she was." Part of him wanted to ask if Lucy believed in him as much as Hope did, but he did not dare. If the answer was *nee*, he knew it would crush him.

* * *

"*Gut* morning," Kanagy said as he strolled into the kitchen the following morning.

"*Gut* morning," Andy said; he could not keep the grin off his face, so he turned back to the stove, stirring the bacon in the pan. He had hardly slept a wink, for he had thought of Hope all night. Half of the night had been full of joy, and the possibilities before them, and the other half was filled with dread and what could go wrong.

"I see you had a *gut* day yesterday." Kanagy shuffled across to the table. "It is *gut* to see a smile on your face. You should do it more often. It suits you."

Andy couldn't help but notice that he seemed stiff this morning, and there was a pallor to his cheeks. Then, he started to cough. Without even thinking about it, Andy put a glass of water next to him.

"You are so *gut* to me," Kanagy said after he finished sipping on the water. The coughing had ceased, but he still looked a little pale.

"How are you feeling?" Worry was like a hole inside Andy. A pit that wanted to open and fill him with

69

despair if he let it. A pit that he feared was filled with Kanagy's death. He pushed the thoughts aside.

"I was so proud to see you yesterday. I want you to know that you are like a son to me and that I love having you here."

Andy served bacon and eggs onto two plates, turning away, for he feared he had smoke in his eyes once more, for they were running. He blinked them rapidly before sitting down at the table. "*Denke*, you have been so *gut* to me that you are like a *daed* to me too. I cannot *denke* enough."

"*Ack*, listen to us like two old washer women." Kanagy took a fork and stabbed at his bacon. "How's the farm doing? Do we have any corn to harvest yet, for the *Englischers* will be here soon?"

Andy was not fooled. He could see moisture in the old man's eyes too. "*Jah*, the first batch will be ready by next weekend. I have already arranged for some to go to market and some to go to the Miller's for their farm store. I will finish the last of the plowing today, and then I will start sewing the oats."

"*Denke*." Kanagy leaned back in his chair and put a hand on his chest. His face went pale and looked a little clammy.

Andy felt a jolt of fear go through him. Was the old man ill? "Are you all right? Do I need to call Dr. Yoder?"

"*Nee*, I am fine. Just a bit of heartburn. You stop worrying and start enjoying your courtship with that wonderful young lady. I can't wait for you to bring her here for dinner."

Andy felt a lump form in his throat. The food he cooked was basic and suitable only for men. He did an okay job, but it was mainly bacon and eggs and the odd casserole. So how could he invite her here? But something else was worrying him. Kanagy had not been as well recently. So he decided that tomorrow when he went for supplies, he would call in and see Dr. Yoder. Maybe the old physician could call around out of the blue?

CHAPTER ELEVEN

* * *

Have I not commanded you?
Be strong and courageous.
Do not be afraid;
do not be discouraged,
for the LORD your God will be with you wherever
you go."
Joshua 1:9

* * *

S till feeling a little worried, Andy made his way out of the *haus*. It was a fresh spring morning, and the sun was already climbing against a clear blue sky. The birds were singing in the trees surrounding the *farmhaus*, and the slight breeze lifted his hat as he made his way to the barn.

Earlier, he had brought in the horses and fed them. Then he groomed them, removing any dirt and ruffled hair while he waited for them to eat. It was a part of the day that he loved, but he also loved plowing. Working with such a powerful team, out in the fresh air, he couldn't think of anything better. Pushing his worries about Kanagy out of his mind, he grabbed the harness and walked to the first stall.

Copper shook his big chestnut head, the flaxen mane and forelock tossed and sent dust motes floating in the sunlight. Andy patted the gentle horse's neck and opened the door, putting on the bridal and harness quickly; he led him outside and tied him up. He repeated the process with Blaze and Red, making sure each horse got plenty of attention. They got a little jealous if they were left out.

Once they were all outside, a robin hopped down from the hedge, and he tossed it a few oats. The bird was a regular and often followed him for a short while. The plow would turn up all sorts of delicious treats. Soon, the larger, more aggressive birds would appear, and the robin would fly off to safety.

The horses made their way to the field at a fast walk, hardly noticing the heavy plow behind them. They were eager to work. "Steady now, boys," he called as he pulled on the reins.

Once in the field, he dropped the plow into the fertile soil below and whispered a prayer of gratitude. It was part of his routine; gratitude always made him feel better, but today he worried about Kanagy. What could he do to help?

The team worked well together, and it was a glorious day. But, before too long, his mind drifted away from Kanagy's health and onto the beautiful Hope. It had seemed a *gut* day yesterday, and she had seemed to enjoy his company. Why was he even doubting this? They had known each other for so long and were always relaxed in each other's company. They never ran out of things to say and wanted the same things out of life. He knew he had to trust himself more, it was just difficult when *nee* one else did.

They had reached the end of the field. He clicked the horses and pulled on the right rein to turn the team for another pass. Once more, they leaned into the breast-plate and enjoyed the work and the sunshine with him. The morning passed quickly and pleasantly in the glorious sunshine. By lunchtime, he would finish the plowing and could start harvesting the corn.

Something caught his eye, and he looked up and back at the farm. Bright lights were flashing there. Was that the sheriff's vehicle, along with two buggies? Fear slipped a knife into his heart. *What was going on? Was Kanagy hurt?*

The horses could not travel that fast, not with a heavy plow behind them. Even so, Andy wanted to push them to a gallop. Something was wrong. Was it Kanagy? The thought of a heart attack went through his mind, and he wondered if to leave the team and run. Or maybe, he could unhitch them and ride one back to the farm. But, instead, he calmed himself, taking a breath and whis-pering a prayer. It was not that far. They would soon be there.

SARAH MILLER

Rushing into the yard, he pulled the horses to a halt and jumped down, tying them to a rail. He noticed that one of the buggies was Bishop Beiler and another was the Glick's buggy. Simon had been here the other day. Was this a coincidence, or did he have something to do with it? ... whatever it was, it worried him.

Another vehicle pulled up, a black van with the word coroner on the side. And his knees nearly gave way. "*Nee*," he screamed and ran forward.

Bishop Beiler stepped in front of him, pulling him into his arms and patting his back. "It is all right, do not worry. He's with *Gott* now."

Andy's eyes were full of tears. "How could this happen? He was fine this morning?" Then he remembered the way Marlin had been clutching his chest. "Was it a heart attack?"

Amos shook his head. "The sheriff thinks it was murder."

Andy sank to his knees. "Murder!"

The next few hours were confusing and heartbreaking for Andy. The sheriff, Peter Buckner, was new to the job. He had become sheriff just last year and was in his early 30s. A tall and thin man with thinning dark hair and serious brown eyes. Andy knew him well. Peter did not like the fact that the Amish lived away from society, as he saw it. Though he was fair and just and believed in the law, he also believed that the Amish dealt with things too much by themselves. Then, of course, he knew Andy's background. The cold stare he was giving Andy sent shivers down his back.

"Sheriff, can I see him. please?" Andy asked.

"No, you need to sit there until I have the time to talk to you." The sheriff's eyes were cold, his words clipped as he turned away and talked to one of his deputies.

"I know it is hard, but do not worry," Amos said. "Sarah and I will be with you throughout this."

"I'm not worried about me. I want to know what happened. Who would murder Old Man Kanagy? Who would murder Marlin? It makes no sense."

"It makes *nee* sense to me either. I do not believe it would be an *Englischer*. He is too far off the beaten track for one to come here. Even if they did, Marlin got on well with everyone. What motive would anyone have?" Amos shook his head, and the sadness in his eyes ran deep. "But, who in our community would do this?" Amos tugged on his beard; his faded blue eyes seemed to shrink into his wrinkled face, and for the first time, he looked old.

"Do not worry," Andy said. "We will discover who did this, and we will get justice."

Behind him, he heard somebody mumbling. "We know who did this. There's only one in this community who is known for violence."

"Maybe this is lucky," another voice added. "The thought of Hope courting that man. It makes my blood run cold."

Andy realized that the bishop had not heard the people gossiping behind them. Undoubtedly, his hearing was not as *gut* as it used to be. However, Andy's was, and he heard and understood every word. He was being blamed for this. Not only had he lost this man who was like a *daed* to him, but he would be accused of killing him. *What could he do?*

The sheriff was free, he walked across, his head high, a confident smile on his face. "Andy Byler, I would like to take you in for questioning over the murder of Marlin Kanagy. Would you come with me, voluntarily, or do I have to arrest you?"

CHAPTER TWELVE

* * *

but those who hope in the LORD will renew their
strength.
They will soar on wings like eagles;
they will run and not grow weary,
they will walk and not be faint.
Isaiah 40:31

* * *

J ust a dash more lavender, Hope thought to herself. The soap mixture already smelled nice, but it needed a little more. She added a few drops of lavender oil and sprinkled in a large pinch of lavender petals. Taking up the two-foot-long wooden spoon, she stirred the mixture dispersing the oil and petals throughout.

Sniffing in, she closed her eyes. It was perfect. It was ready. Now all she had to do was pour it into a large flat tin, and then, once it was set, she would cut it into squares and prepare it for sale. Today had been a *gut* day. A smile crossed her face, as they had tended to do all morning. She would be working and realize that she was grinning from ear to ear.

Going to service with Andy yesterday was wonderful. Sure, at first, there had been a few mutterings and mumblings from those who believed he was evil. However, Bishop Beiler soon stopped that. She smiled as she thought about Andy's sweet face and the way he blushed when he looked at her.

They had arranged to go on a picnic Wednesday evening. The nights were drawing out now, and it was warm enough to do so. *Where would he take her?*

The sound of horse hooves coming in fast outside her workshop made her look up. Her *daed* had made this room at the back of the *haus* for her to prepare her soap. It was perfect, but she could not see the front of the *haus*, only the side. Stressed voices filled the air. It

SARAH MILLER

sounded a little like her parents, but they were too far away for her to be sure.

Quickly, she poured the soap into the tray and scraped out the mixing drum. At this stage, she could leave it for a while and see who had arrived at the *haus*. A touch of joy ran through her. Could it be Andy?

When she came out of her workshop, she was surprised to see her *mamm* and *daed* rushing toward her. But then, the joy was replaced with fear. What had happened?

"Do not worry," Anna said.

"*Mamm*, saying that will make me worry. What is wrong?" Anna clenched her hands together and felt soap setting on her fingers. It crumbled off and dropped to the floor as she clung onto her apron.

"It's Andy," her *daed* removed his hat and scrunched the rim in his hands. "Well, it's Old Man Kanagy. He's dead."

Hope felt her hands fly to her face as her heart broke. She knew how much Andy loved the old man. She cared for him deeply too. "How, when?"

A look passed between her *mamm* and her *daed*. They were hiding something. *What was it?*

Samuel bowed his head for a moment, and when he raised it, his lips were drawn in a tight line. "I may as well tell you. The sheriff thinks he was murdered... and he thinks it might have been Andy."

"*Nee, nee,* he wouldn't do that. Andy loves him, and he never did what people say he did. You have to believe him." Hope could see that her parents didn't. Their eyes were full of pity for her, or sadness for Marlin Kanagy, and possibly even a bit of relief that Andy would be out of her way. "I can't believe you don't trust him. All the years he spent in our *haus.* You know him!" Hope knew that her voice had risen and that her cheeks were flushed. Emotions were whirling around her like a tornado. There was sorrow and anger and fear and desperation. She had to grab onto one of them, and she feared that it might be anger.

Her *mamm* held out her hands and took Hope's in hers. "It is not that we don't believe him. We certainly believe and trust you."

"Then help me prove he is innocent." Once more, she saw a look pass between her parents and realized they had simply been humoring her.

"We have to let the Lord do His job," Samuel said.

"Do you believe he is innocent?" Hope pulled her hands free and clasped them behind her back. She could see the doubt on her parents' faces. Could see that they wanted to say *jah,* but they couldn't. "Will you help me prove his innocence?"

Her *mamm* shook her head.

It was too much. Hope turned and ran. With tears streaming down her cheeks, she ran across the rough ground behind the *haus,* over the lane, and into the field. She would find peace and quiet in the woods nearby, and maybe she could think of a plan. Andy was innocent. She was going to save him. But what if *nee* one else believed him? Would he spend his life behind bars?

Hope ran for what seemed like forever, but gradually she slowed down. She was breathless. Crying and running was not the easiest thing to do. She had to think. There had to be some way to prove that Andy didn't do this. She knew he could not have done it. Partly because she knew him but also because she had seen him working in the fields all morning.

Whenever she took a break, she walked out to the fence and watched him plowing.

It was a wonderful sight. He was tall and strong, and the horse's chestnut coats and flaxen manes and tails against the dark earth made a stunning picture. Then there were the birds circling behind him. It reminded her of one of the pictures that Emma King painted. It was beautiful, stunning, she could have watched him all day; why didn't she? If she had been, she could be his alibi. Maybe she could, anyway. She was only ever in the workshop for up to an hour. How long did it take to murder someone?

She shuddered as she had another thought. Poor Marlin. He did not deserve this. Sobbing once more, she stopped and slumped to the ground and prayed for his soul. Maybe she should go home and talk to her parents or Bishop Beiler. There had to be some way of saving Andy and finding out who had committed this crime.

Then she thought of all the horrible things she had heard at service on Sunday. Too many people would believe he had done this. They were foolish and selfish. She was angry at them. Why couldn't they see the man he really was?

Part of her wanted to run and shake them and tell them they were wrong. But, that would do *nee gut*. She had *nee* way of saving Andy, and she had to find one.

Lowering her head and clasping her hands together, she began to pray. Then, maybe, *Gott* would show her the way. She had to trust in Him, for she knew that Andy was innocent.

CHAPTER THIRTEEN

* * *

I keep my eyes always on the LORD.
With him at my right hand, I will not be shaken.
Psalm 16:8

* * *

"I just wish I had done something earlier," Simon Glick said. His head was held high, his chin jutting out, and he swaggered a bit as he walked with some of the men of Faith's Creek. "As I said, I saw Andy going into the barn about an hour ago." Simon shook his head, hoping it looked dramatic. "If only I had done something... I could have saved...." What could he call the old man? Awkward, annoying. "A much-loved member of our district. If only."

"*Nee*, none of us would have thought this could happen," James Schrock said. "We all thought he loved Kanagy."

They were making their way back to their buggies. The sheriff had gone, and he had taken Andy away. The bishop had told them all to go home. But Simon was not ready to, yet. He had another job to do, but he couldn't do it while these people were here.

"I just wish I had run in there and stopped that evil man." Simon bowed his head to hide a grin.

"You would've been a hero," Henry Esch said.

Simon felt himself stand a little taller. Part of him wanted to get rid of the men, but maybe he should milk this a little more.

"Well, don't worry. Our family will keep the farm going until this is sorted."

"As it should be," a man said.

Simon noticed that Bishop Amos was watching them. "I guess we should be on our way." Nodding at them all, he climbed into his buggy. It took all his self-control to not whip the horse and race out of there. Still, his *daed* would get angry if he got in trouble with the bishop, again.

As the horse trotted along the lane, he watched Amos's buggy pull out of the farm and turn in the opposite direction. That was *gut*. Whipping the horse, he increased the speed. Now he would have to drive around in a circle to return to the farm. This was so annoying. Why did it have to be so complicated? Why couldn't people just do as they were told?

Then he realized complicated was better. There was *nee* way he could conduct this business with his *daed* watching.

Hope was finding it hard to concentrate on her prayers. The ground was slightly damp, and the leaves tickled her feet. Sunlight filtered through the leaves, dappling against the woodland floor. It was too nice here. She wanted it to be anything but. It seemed wrong for the sun to shine when Andy was in such trouble and Old Man Kanagy lay dead.

Scrunching her eyes even tighter, she tried to pray once more, but a noise interrupted her. *What was that?* A pitiful cry came across the silent woodland, stroking cold hands down her spine. She glanced around but could see nothing. *Where had the noise come from, and what was it?*

It was *nee* use. Hope knew that when her prayers wouldn't come, there was *nee* point in forcing them. Luckily, it was unusual for her. Prayer usually gave her such comfort and often the answer she needed. There, the sound came again. This time it was easier to hear. Something or someone was in pain.

Leaping to her feet, she listened and strained her ears to pick up the noise. There, she heard it again. It was weak and pitiful, but she had the direction and set off toward it.

The noise came again, and she started to run. The forest floor was covered in sticks, and one sharp one made her cry out as it dug into her foot, but she wouldn't stop. Not when someone was in need. As she came around a large tree, the sight before her made her increase her speed. *Who could do such a thing?*

Sprinting the last few feet, she dropped to her knees to see a small, fluffy golden dog caught in a snare. Anger ran through her, replaced by fear, as the dog snapped at her. Sharp teeth came so close to her fingers. She stepped back quickly. The dog whimpered again and looked at her with big brown sorrowful eyes. It was obvious that the poor creature had been there some time. It was thin, its coat matted and straggly, and its left rear leg was covered in blood. *What could she do? Was there a way to save it? Would it let her?*

Simon had done a short-circuit in his buggy and returned to Kanagy's farm. He glanced around, but it seemed that *nee* one was here. If anyone said anything, he would just make an excuse that he forgot something or wanted to check on something. Then, he could use it to put more blame on Andy.

The coast seemed clear, so he jumped down and patted his pocket. The thick envelope was still there. *Gut*, it was best that he got this over and done as quickly as possible. Right now, he wanted to be far away from here and what had happened.

Quickly, he made his way into the woods. He wanted this final stage complete, so he could put the next part of the plan into action. Maybe once this was done, his *daed* would think he was worthy. Maybe, but he doubted it.

The meeting place, in the woods, was just a short walk, but each step made him feel vulnerable and worried. After all, he was meeting a murderer. What if the man changed his mind, wanted more money, or what if he wanted to leave *nee* witnesses? Simon stopped. Should he just run out of here and forget it? *Nee*, if he did that, then Brad might talk. Apart from that, he was a good 6 inches taller than the man who had done his dirty work. If this went wrong, then it was Brad who needed to worry.

Simon glanced behind him once more. The wood seemed awfully quiet and cold. Was it always this cold under the trees? He chuckled. Of course, it was because the sunlight couldn't penetrate as easily. He was just being silly. He was behaving like his *daed* always told him he did. He was being weak and foolish.

"I was beginning to think you weren't coming," a deep voice said off to his left.

Simon's heart began to pound against his chest, and he turned suddenly, raising his arms in front of him. It was evident from the movement that he was afraid. The last thing he needed to do was show weakness. This man might take advantage of it.

"I had to make sure that no one saw me. So, let's get this over and done with, and then I don't want to see you again, ever."

Brad Henderson was standing beneath a large oak tree. Its leaves and branches spread out above him, casting what looked like a spotlight across his face. The man was wiry, only about 5 foot six, with wispy brown hair and the meanest brown eyes that Simon had ever seen. It was those eyes that had drawn the two of them together. Those eyes that had pulled Simon to talk to the man across the crowded bar. He knew his *daed* would hate it if he realized that he still went drinking, but he had struggled to give it up. In the end, he didn't see the point. It hurt *nee* one and gave him a little peace.

Brad had become a friend. They thought the same way and had been dealt equally rough deals. So, when he joked about wanting to get rid of Marlin Kanagy, Brad had made him an offer.

Brad chuckled. "I guess you're going to stay out of the alehouse then, huh."

The thought was not a *gut* one. Drinking was his one escape. "Maybe; if not, I suggest we don't talk to each other."

"Just give me what I'm owed." Brad shook his head. "Then, if we run into each other again, don't act squirrelly. There's nothing more suspicious than someone changing their behavior."

Simon hated it when somebody told him what to do. He knew what was best. He would keep away from this man from now on. Suddenly, he didn't want to pay, but the look in Brad's eyes told him he had to.

Reaching back, he pulled the envelope from out of his pocket. It was probably the best $5000 he had ever spent. There was nothing to stop him from getting the farm now. He noticed how Brad's mean eyes widened, and the shorter man licked his lips as he looked at the money. Simon almost handed it over, but at the last second, he pulled it away. "Remember our deal. This never happened."

Brad nodded.

"Was it hard?" He didn't know why he had to ask that.

Brad chuckled. "It was easy. He didn't know what hit him?" Brad's voice raised as he said the words, and the look in his eyes was manic. Then, his arm shot out, and he snatched the money. The speed with which he moved left Simon breathless.

"Don't worry, I won't say a word." With that, Brad turned, stared into the woods momentarily, and disappeared into the forest.

Simon felt nervous; he wanted to get out of there but thought he heard something behind him. *Was that a stick breaking? Was someone there?* He turned and stared into the woods. *Who was out here? Had they heard him?* If so, he would have to deal with them, harshly.

CHAPTER FOURTEEN

* * *

31 For no one is cast off by the Lord forever.
32 Though he brings grief, he will show compassion,
so great is his unfailing love.
Lamentations 3:31-32

* * *

H ope sat down a little way away from the dog. It breathed a sigh of relief and seemed to relax. However, its eyes were still wary, and it licked its lips.

"You must be starving," she whispered as soothingly as she could. "You must be in such a lot of pain and so afraid, but I won't hurt you." She smoothed her apron and felt something inside it. She had placed a cookie in there earlier, wrapped in greaseproof paper. Perhaps, she could use this as a bribe and win the dog over to her.

Slowly, she took the package out of her apron and unwrapped it. The dog raised his nose and sniffed. Its eyes looked a little brighter. It almost looked apologetic, but she did not dare approach, not yet. There were two cookies inside the package, they were oat cookies, and she didn't know if they were *gut* for dogs or not. However, looking at the poor thing, it was obvious that anything was better than nothing.

She broke the first cookie into eight pieces and held a bit up, letting the dog look at it. Once more, the little dog raised its head and sniffed the air. It whined again, but this time it sounded more like a plea. The little dog was the size of a miniature poodle, but it was clearly a cross-breed of some sort. The coat was honey-colored and curly like a poodle, but the dog was too stocky. Or it would be once it had some meat on its bones. She couldn't work out which one, or maybe it was many.

"This is *gut*. You would like it." She tossed a little bit as close to the dog as she could.

As fast as lightning, it reached out and gobbled down the morsel. Then, from beneath it, a ragged and matted tail appeared and wagged slowly.

"There, you see, we can become friends." She threw another piece of cookie, and this time, the dog caught it. Its tail wagged a little more.

Over the next 20 to 30 minutes, she fed the dog most of the cookies, gradually moving closer and closer. Finally, when she was down to the last few pieces, she reached out her hand. At first, the dog shrank back. Hope froze but held her hand where it was, and after a few moments, the dog reached up and sniffed her fingers. Then, he licked them.

Hope reached out and stroked him, and at first, he shied away, but then he leaned into her hand. "It seems like you have known kindness," she said as she ran her hand down his body. Beneath her fingers, his ribs protruded through his skin. His coat was thick and matted with dirt. As she moved her hand down to his leg, he whined slightly but let her go closer. Some of the blood had dried, but the wound was still open and sore, even though it wasn't really bleeding.

She glanced around her and traced the snare back to where it was hammered into the ground. Getting it off the dog would be easier if she could remove it at that point, but she was still a little worried. If she hurt him, would he bite her?

Slowly, gently, she worked her way around to the edge of the snare. There was no way she could remove the wire from the peg that hammered it into the ground. Then, maybe, she could get the peg out. However, it didn't seem likely. This dog had been here for some time and had *nee* doubt thrown everything he had into getting loose. It hadn't worked.

She grabbed hold of the peg and tried to rock it from side to side, hoping to loosen its hold in the ground. It wasn't moving. Maybe she should go home and come back with some bolt croppers? Only she didn't want to leave him alone. If she did, she feared that he would think he was abandoned once more. It would break her heart to do that to him.

Looking around, she tried to see something she could dig with. There was nothing. The few bits of branch and wood were too rotten or old. They would not make a digging implement.

Closing her eyes, she tried to think, then felt a soft touch on her arm and opened her eyes to see that the dog had moved toward her. It was resting its nose on her arm and looking at her with eyes full of hope. She almost let out a whoop of joy for doing so had loosened the wire. Luckily, she stopped herself, for if she had done so, she feared she would have scared him, and he would've pulled away, tightening the wire. Gently, she moved so that his head was nestled on her lap. He sighed and closed his eyes.

Could she reach the wire? The leg with the wire was out behind him, and she could see the wire was looser than before. With luck, she could free him without causing too much pain.

"Now, let me help you," she said softly, slipping her hand down his back and leg. Gradually, slowly, she moved. She felt him tense and held her breath. This was so close. Her fingers touched the wire, and she felt him stiffen. "It's okay, little man. I'm trying to help you."

He whined again, and she moved her hand away, freezing until she felt him relax. This time, she moved quickly, freed up the wire from his matted fur, and made it into a big loop. Now, all she had to do was move his leg from it. But how?

The dog looked up at her, and then he pulled his leg free. He jumped up, barked, and looked off into the woods.

"Stay with me," she said and offered him the last piece of cookie.

The dog sniffed from a distance and looked at her with sad eyes before turning and racing away.

"Hey, dog, come back."

It was *nee gut*. He was gone.

Andy stared across the table in what he knew was an interrogation room. The sheriff had not said a word since he sat down over 5 minutes ago. All he was doing was reading a file, and it made Andy nervous. He wanted to go home, to talk to Hope, to see the bishop. But, most of all, he wanted Kanagy to be alive and to see him once more.

This room was so empty, with its grey walls and basic furniture. A red light flashed on a device above. He presumed it was a camera, having seen a bit of television while on his *rumspringa*. He knew what was going on;

the sheriff was sweating him. The man was acting cool, in charge, and hoping that he would get nervous and blurt out a confession. Only, he had nothing to confess.

The sheriff looked up. Those eyes seemed cold now and all-seeing. As if they could pierce through to Andy's very soul.

Sheriff Buckner smiled, but there was nothing warm or reassuring about it. It was the smile of a spider to a fly, of a coyote to a rabbit, or a lawman to a villain. So, even though he hated himself, Andy couldn't help but look away.

"Now, son, tell me what happened." The sheriff's voice was calm, reassuring, and almost lulled Andy into talking.

"I was plowing. I looked up and saw the lights flashing and buggies. So I raced across and... and...." A lump filled his throat, and tears ran down his cheeks. "Is he really dead?"

"He certainly is. I reckon you beat him a good ten times. He put up a good fight but couldn't stand against your frenzied attack."

"Oh, my *Gott, nee.*"

"What?"

"I can't believe this; who would do such a thing?"

The sheriff smiled. A crocodile smile. "I guess it would be someone who had just found out he was losing his job and his home."

"Who was that?" Andy asked, confused.

"You," the sheriff said, "don't deny it. Simon told us everything."

Andy felt a sickness inside. What had Simon done?

CHAPTER FIFTEEN

* * *

4 I have no greater joy than to hear
that my children are walking in the truth.
John 1:4

* * *

Hope watched the dog disappear through the trees and wondered what to do. Should she follow him, or should she just go home? The problem was, if she went home, she had to face the truth, and she couldn't do that, not now. Besides, the dog needed her.

She set off across the forest in the direction she had seen it go. It was heading back toward Faith's Creek, probably back towards the Kanagy farm, or at least in that general direction.

Stepping lightly, she went as quickly as possible and almost jogged after the dog. *How far had she walked into the forest? How far did she need to go back?* For a moment, a shiver of fear went down her spine. *What if she got lost?*

Pushing the thought aside, she kept walking and walking, and then she saw the dog standing just ahead of her. He was staring at something, but she couldn't see what. Whatever it was, she could see that his hackles were up and his teeth were bared. Should she turn and run?

"Hey, boy," she whispered.

The dog turned around and saw her. Then, wagging his tail, he approached her and stood between her and whatever he had been looking at. It was almost as if he was protecting her, and she ran a hand down his back and felt his tail wag even more.

"Here," she said and handed him the final bit of cookie.

He wolfed it down but didn't move. Then she could hear voices. They were faint, but two separate men were talking. Slipping around the dog, she went from tree to tree getting closer and closer to the voices.

When there were just a few trees and bushes between her and the strangers, she stopped. Standing in front of her were two men. One was Simon Glick, and he looked nervous as if he was posturing. Neither of those two things was unusual. Though he was arrogant and always angry, she often thought it was because he was afraid. The other man she didn't know; he was much shorter than Simon. They were facing each other side onto her. All she could see of the second man was that he was short with a wiry build and had wispy brown hair. Yet, there was something confident about him. It made her feel uneasy. He was undoubtedly the alpha between the two of them.

Hope felt something touch her, and she looked down to see the dog leaning against her side. He looked worried and as if he wanted to run. Gently, she stroked his head, and he leaned into her. She tried to reassure him but didn't dare move or say a word in case the two men heard her. Whatever they were doing, she doubted it was anything *gut*.

She couldn't really make out any words, but as she watched, Simon pulled a large envelope out of his pocket and held it up. It was as if he was negotiating or making a point. Quietly, she moved a little closer, going from one tree to another. Then, finally, she stopped behind a bush and peered through the leaves.

"Was it hard?" Simon asked, and Hope felt a sick feeling inside of her.

"It was easy. He didn't know what hit him," the other man said, and then his hand shot out, and he took the envelope. Though she couldn't see what was in it, Hope had a feeling that it was filled with money. *How could she even think that? What was going on here? Had she just heard that man confessing to killing Kanagy?*

Before she could even think about it, the smaller man turned and stared right at her. Freezing, her heart hammered against her chest until he melted into the trees. Then, as Simon turned, the dog stepped back and broke a twig. The noise seemed to reverberate through the woods, even though she knew it was but a slight snap.

Simon looked around. Had he seen them? Would he come after them? That was when she understood. This had to be a payoff. *Had Simon paid to have Kanagy killed, and if so, why?*

Simon searched the bushes, and the dog whined before running off into the trees. He looked back. *Was he begging her to follow him? Dare she move? If she did, would Simon find her, and would he kill her too?*

* * *

The urge to throw up was overwhelming, and Andy found himself swallowing and gasping for breath as he tried to stop himself. Had Simon had something to do with this? The man was telling lies. He couldn't have had Kanagy killed, could he?

"I see the fact that I know about your situation has shocked you," the sheriff said.

Andy had heard him talking, but his brain didn't grasp the words.

The sheriff banged his fist on the table. "Look at me. A man is dead. Admit to killing him, and it will go easier for you. You might even see daylight again, one day."

Andy swallowed and took a deep breath. He knew that Kanagy would not want him to panic. That his mentor and his friend would want him to think carefully and sensibly about this and work out what had happened. Closing his eyes, Andy whispered a prayer, and then raising his head, he looked directly at the sheriff. "Forgive me; I am shocked at my friend's death and finding it hard to comprehend what is happening. I didn't hear what you said."

A look flashed behind the sheriff's eyes. Did he believe him?

"Could you please tell me what you just said?" Andy asked.

The sheriff didn't look quite as sure of himself; he nodded. "What I wanted to know was... were you angry when you found out that you were losing your job and your home?"

Andy felt as if he was back in the *Englischer* world and had had one too many to drink. "I don't understand you."

"Simon told us about his deal to buy the farm." The sheriff folded his arms and sat back. His hard eyes stared into Andy. He was trying to see what reaction this news would have.

"Marlin told me that Simon had called and made an offer for the farm. He also told me he didn't want to sell. It was his home, and he wanted to live there for as long as he could. I loved him...." A lump formed in Andy's throat, and he had to swallow hard to fight back the tears. Somehow, he didn't think that the sheriff would treat them with sympathy.

"Simon also said he saw you going into the barn. He wishes he had come in and stopped you. What do you say to that?"

"Of course, I went into the barn. I feed the horses, milk and feed the cow, and then I groom them and harness them for the work for the day. I go into the barn multiple times every day, but this morning, it was just after breakfast the last time I went in there."

"And what time was that?"

Panic rushed through Andy, for he had not looked at the clock. He rarely did, for he worked with the sun and daylight. "I don't know, but I had been plowing for maybe three hours when I saw your car." An awful feeling came over him. How long had Kanagy been lying there? If he had come back earlier, could he have done something? "Could I have saved him?"

A look of shock crossed the sheriff's face. "If you had stopped your beating, then yes, you could've."

"Beating!" Andy dropped his head as a flood of tears left his eyes and dripped onto the table. *Nee* matter what happened, he had let his friend down. He should've been there for him.

"Simon told us that he saw you leaving the barn about half an hour before he found the body. Why were you in the barn, at that time, and did you see anything?"

"Simon found the body?" Andy looked up and saw doubt in the sheriff's eyes.

"Yes, he did."

"Don't you think that is suspicious?" Andy could see more doubt, but then he watched as anger crossed the sheriff's face.

"My problem is, Simon Glick has never been in trouble with the law, but you...." His hand tapped on the file in front of him, "You have quite a record. I will leave you to think on that for a while, and when you want to tell me what really happened, then maybe we can talk."

Andy watched the sheriff get up and walk out of the room. A sense of devastation washed over him. His friend was dead, and there was nothing he could do. It looked like he would be blamed for the murder while the real killer went free.

CHAPTER SIXTEEN

* * *

Blessed is the one who does not walk in step with the wicked or stand in the way that sinners take or sit in the company of mockers,
Psalm 1:1

* * *

Hope froze until Simon disappeared between the trees. Letting out a breath as the bushes waved in the air behind him. He had gone! Or at least she hoped he had. What if he was circling around and coming after her?

Heart pounding, she looked around for the dog, but it was also gone. A pain shot through her, and she felt weak. This was all too much. She wanted to cry, scream, and call for the dog, but she was scared in case Simon heard her. *What could she do?* Fear pushed her to run. She raced through the forest, jumping over fallen logs and being whipped by branches. It felt like the devil was on her heels, and her mind imagined Simon grabbing her shoulder and pulling her around.

At last, she stopped. Breathless, panting, her emotions took over. The world felt cold and desolate. *What could she do?*

In the end, she sank to the forest floor and prayed. This time, the prayer was easier. She asked that Andy would be released, that Simon would pay for any sins he committed, and that she found the dog. She asked if she should go to the police, but it was Bishop Beiler's face that came to her mind. Saying amen, she got up. She could look for the dog later. Maybe, this information would help Andy and Amos Beiler would know what to do. He always did.

It seemed to take forever for her to make her way out of the forest and along the lane to the bishop's *haus*. It didn't; it just seemed that way. With every step, she expected to see Simon. Fear had her whipping around at each bird call or noise from leaves in the trees. It sounded like they were whispering behind her, colluding to bring her down.

Stop it, she told herself. *You are safe. But was she?*

She was eager to help Andy and then go in search of the dog. But who did he belong to? Would she find him again? The ragged little creature had been a beacon of hope on a horrid day.

At last, she cleared the trees and felt her feet cushioned by the soft grass. It was warm between her toes, giving her a sense of freedom. She was safe.

The rays of the sun warmed her as she walked along the lane. Still, she hurried as the birds sang in the hedgerow and the breeze tugged at her *kapp*. It all seemed so normal, but everything had changed.

As she approached the bishop's *haus*, she saw something lying in the road. Her heart jumped in her chest. It was the dog. Oh, *nee*, this was more than she could take. Had he been run over? Racing to him, she called out, "Help me, please help me."

Dropping to her knees, she gently touched the dog's side. He cried, and she stroked his matted fur. "You are okay," she said just as Amos arrived at her side.

"Oh, my, what happened?" he asked.

"I found him in the woods in a snare," she said through tears. "I got him free, but I saw and heard something, and he ran away. There is something I must tell you, but can we help him first?"

"I will fetch my buggy. I was just going out, so I won't be long. We will take him to see Abel, your Aunt Katie's son."

Hope nodded, but Amos had already gone. She tried to check the dog over but could see nothing wrong except the damaged paw. *It looked a mess, but what had happened to him, and where was he going?*

Amos was back with the buggy and jumped down with a blanket. Hope wrapped it gently around the dog and lifted him into the buggy.

As they trotted along the road, she prayed that the dog would survive. She was pleased that she had found him near Amos's. The bishop always knew what to do. Her cousin, Abel was just like his *mamm*, Katie. He loved animals and was training to be a veterinarian. Hope prayed that he could help. She did not think she could cope if she lost this poor animal.

Soon, Abel was tending to the dog, and Amos and Hope were drinking *kaffe* at her Aunt Katie's table. It was a big oak table in a large but sparse kitchen. Katie spent more time with her horses than baking and cooking. On the side was a ledger. Her Uncle Eli did the books for many of the district. Usually, he worked in his office overlooking the river, but sometimes, she knew he worked at this table.

Hope pulled her eyes off the red and worn cover of the book. She knew she was distracting herself, looking at the mundane to avoid facing the present.

Katie had realized that the bishop wanted to talk to Hope and had left them to it, no doubt, going to her stables.

"Do you think he will be okay?" Hope asked.

"Abel seemed sure he would be." Amos sipped his *kaffe*, his faded blue eyes watching her.

"I forget what he said." Hope shrugged. She had been so worried that she hadn't heard anything Abel had told her.

Amos smiled. "I understand. He said the dog was dehydrated and probably collapsed due to that and a lack of blood. Possibly even an infection. He told you he would treat the wound, give him blood and antibiotics, and that he would be fine in an hour or two."

"*Denke*," Hope said. "I saw something in the woods. I think I should go to the police."

"What did you see?"

As they drank *kaffe* and nibbled on cookies from her own parents' bakery, Hope explained how she had fought with her parents and run into the woods. How she prayed and heard the dog and freed him. Then she told him about seeing Simon give money to the man.

"Are you sure it was money?" Amos asked.

Hope blushed a little. "It was a thick envelope. It must have been money. I think he paid that man to kill Kanagy."

Amos's eyes widened, but he hid his emotions well. "You can't know that. I agree that what you said is worth looking into, but there is *nee* proof here."

Hope felt drained at those words. She had expected the bishop to be ecstatic to hear this and to take her to the sheriff. She had expected Andy to be coming home tonight, but from the look on Amos's face, that would not happen.

Hope was fighting back the tears when the door opened. Abel came through with the dog on a lead. The little creature looked much better, much brighter, and his tail was waving through the air. "This little one sure is a fighter," Abel said. "Who does he belong to? I would like to have a word with them about his treatment?"

"I found him in a snare," Hope said, even though she had already told him this.

"I think he is a stray," Amos said.

"Not anymore," Hope was shaking her head. He was not going to the pound. "He's mine."

Amos grinned and nodded.

"Then what is his name?" Abel was smiling, and she knew he was teasing her. He knew she didn't know the dog's name, but then she did. It came to her in an instant. Even if it was his new name, he now had one. "His name is Truth, for he led me to it."

"Truth, I like it," Abel said. "He is going to be okay. He is thin and needs a good meal and some rest. These are antibiotics, the instructions are on the package, and I will see him again in a few days."

"*Denke*, Abel." She went over and picked up the dog. She was not letting him go anytime soon. "Amos, would you take me to see the sheriff. Please?"

"Of course. Just don't expect too much."

Hope nodded, but it didn't matter. She knew who the killer was, and if the sheriff wouldn't help her, she would find the evidence herself.

CHAPTER SEVENTEEN

* * *

17 Therefore, if anyone is in Christ,
he is a new creation;
the old has gone,
the new has come!
2 Corinthians 5:17

* * *

The gentle rocking of the buggy soothed Hope's nerves as they made their way towards the sheriff's station at Bird-in-Hand. Truth was nestled on the seat between them. For once, the bishop had been unusually quiet. Perhaps he was allowing her to think, or perhaps he was thinking himself. At first, it made Hope feel better, but now she was becoming nervous. It would take them the best part of an hour to traverse the 7-mile journey. It was a long time for her to worry and work herself up into a panic. Amos's horse was fit and fast, but even so, today, she wished to be there in an instant.

"What I heard, it must be proof. Andy has to come home. We both know he didn't do this." Hope hated that her voice sounded so unsure. It was whiny and childish.

"I wish that were true," Amos said. "Unfortunately, it is only your word against Simon's."

"But it is the truth," she blurted the words out in a sob, not giving him a chance to finish. She hated herself for being so weak.

Amos turned to look at her and smiled. "I believe you. I really do believe you, and I will do everything in my power to see Andy free and his reputation restored. We must pray on this and ask for answers. However, we cannot expect the sheriff to treat him differently than he would anyone else."

Hope sighed and felt Truth touch her leg with his nose. It was comforting. She reached down and stroked his fur. Abel had cleaned some of the matting from it, but she had a lot more to do. Once she got home, she would give him a bath and trim out the worst of the burrs. Then a thought struck her. *How would she tell her parents? Would they let her keep him? Why was life so complicated?*

For a while, she stared out of the window and watched the fields go by. Worrying would not make the journey go quicker, so eventually, she closed her eyes to pray.

Quicker than she expected, Amos pulled the horse into a parking space and stopped. "Let me do the talking," he said, squeezing her shoulder.

She nodded but knew it would be hard to hold her tongue. A smile flickered across her lips as she remembered one of her *mamm's* favorite sayings when she was young and challenging. "I'll tie a knot in that tongue if you don't stop it wagging." It had always been said in humor, but her *mamm* understood that she struggled to stay quiet. Especially when she believed in something.

Soon, they were in the sheriff's office. He had a large desk that seemed too clean and tidy for her liking. There was a screen on one side, and occasionally he tapped away at the keyboard and stared at it as if it was the font of all knowledge. The only other thing on his desk was a phone, a *kaffe* mug on a coaster, and Andy's file.

"I do not think this is even relevant," the sheriff said. "You probably just saw two people making a business arrangement. Now, we have a killer." He tapped his pen on Andy's file. "He has a motive, opportunity, and means. He has a history of aggression and violent behavior. In my mind, we have the right man."

Hope stood and clasped her hands onto the polished wooden desk. "I heard them discussing this. And Simon, Simon is much more likely to kill someone than the sweet and kind Andy."

The sheriff leaned back in his oversized leather chair, which tilted with him. For a moment, she thought he might fall. For a moment, she was pleased. *What would the bishop think?* Heat flushed her cheeks, and she bowed her head.

He placed his hands behind his head and gave a smile that was more of a smirk. "I see what's going on here. You're sweet on this boy. Don't worry; it happens all the time. A few compliments whispered in your ear, and you will believe anything. Trust me, it is to your benefit that he stays behind bars. Now, I have work to do." He stood up and escorted them to the door.

Hope felt the bishop's hand on her shoulder as they made their way back to the buggy. She couldn't look at him, couldn't speak. If she did, she knew that the tears would fall. How could that stupid man not believe her? It made no sense. In her mind, the evidence was clear, yet Andy was no nearer to freedom.

"Do not take this to heart," Bishop Amos said. "That man's attitude was my reason for tempering your expectations. I believe you. Though Jacob Glick has grown and become an acceptable member of our district, his son still has a long way to go."

Amos patted the horse's neck and opened the door offering Hope his hand to climb inside. The look on his face was one of understanding and sympathy, but she thought she saw determination there too. She hoped so.

As she slid onto the seat, Truth squirmed across to her and laid his nose on her leg. It made her feel better; at least the dog believed in her.

On the long journey back, Hope and Amos discussed what they could do.

"We need to identify this man," Amos said.

"Perhaps I could describe him to Emma Byler. Hope shrugged her shoulders. She had *nee* idea if this was possible and if Emma would be able to create a picture of the man she had seen from her recollections. Could she even describe him? She had only really seen his face, straight on, once, and he had been at a fair distance. However, he was an *Englischer*. If she could get a likeness, and if he visited the district at all, someone would know who he was.

It was something, the only thing they had at the moment.

They arrived at her home, and Amos helped her out of the buggy. Before he left, he put a hand on her shoulder and looked her in the eyes. "Be patient, I will not let this go, but it might take time. Do not confront Simon. It could be dangerous. If he knows you suspect this...." Amos paused.

Hope felt a touch of fear run down her spine. He was saying that she could be next. That Simon would kill her to keep his secret. "I understand," she said, her voice shaking just a little.

"Pray on it, and I will do the same."

Hope nodded and watched him drive away. Truth was nuzzling at her leg. Even though she still had him on a leash, he didn't seem to want to leave her anymore. It looked like she had made a friend.

"Hope," she heard her *mamm* call. The note of alarm in her voice was clear, and Hope realized how long she had been gone. It would soon be dark. She had run out in anger. Her parents must have been frantic. "Where have you been? We've been worried about you."

Anna came running over, and Hope's heart was filled with another fear. *Would they let her keep the dog?*

Before she could say anything, she was pulled into her *mamm's* arms and hugged. It felt *gut*. She leaned into the hug and let her tears fall.

"There, there, it is all right. I know it hurts, but you will get over this," Anna said as she ran her hand in circles over Hope's back.

"I want justice, *Mamm*. Andy deserves it."

"Of course, of course. We will help in any way we can, but you have to let the police do their work. Now, come on in. I have a casserole keeping warm for you and some nice fresh bread."

"Okay, *Mamm*, but I have something else to tell you." She could feel Truth leaning against her leg. He was shivering. Possibly afraid of the new people or of what would happen next.

Anna pulled back, looked at her, and then noticed the dog at Hope's feet for the first time. A look of shock came over her face.

Hope wondered if there would be a fight. It didn't matter. She was keeping Truth.

CHAPTER EIGHTEEN

* * *

Because of the LORD's great love we are not consumed,
for his compassions never fail.
23 They are new every morning;
great is your faithfulness.
Lamentations 3:22-23

* * *

A nna's mouth dropped open as her eyes alighted on the dog at Hope's feet. "What is that?"

If it hadn't been so scary, Hope would have laughed. But the thought that her *mamm* might not allow the dog in the *haus* sent a shiver down her spine. "He is my dog, Truth," Hope said, reaching down and stroking the little dog's head.

"Your dog! Your dog.... Where did it come from? Does it have fleas? I... I...."

The door to the *haushold* opened, and they both turned to see Samuel running toward her. "Hope, I am so pleased you are all right. We have been worried sick." He pulled her into his arms, picked her off the ground, and spun her around. "*Dochder*, do not do this to me ever again. My heart can't take it." He put her down and stepped back, holding a hand over his heart and feigning pain.

"Sorry, *Daed*, it was not my intention. I was angry. But maybe, maybe, I was meant to run away because it brought me to the truth."

"What do you mean?" Anna asked.

Before Hope could answer, she noticed the expression on her *daed's* face. His eyes were wide, and a smile curled his lips. "Who is this little fella?" Before Hope could answer, he had dropped to his knees and pulled the dog into a cuddle.

At first, Truth was unsure. But soon, he realized that this human was *gut*. The little dog squirmed in Samuel's arms, and he was laughing with delight. He looked up at Hope. "Does he have a name?"

"I called him Truth, because he led me to it."

Samuel picked the dog up and put his hand on Hope's shoulder. "Come on inside, let's get you some food in your belly, and this little man looks like he could do with a bath. You can then tell us all about him."

Hope snuck a look at her *mamm*. Anna shrugged and gave her a smile. It looked like Truth was staying, and she couldn't be happier. Now, all she had to do was prove that Andy was innocent.

Hope was frustrated. Things took so long. By the time she had explained everything to her parents, eaten a meal, and bathed Truth, it was dark. It was too late to go and see Emma. It caused her more frustration because she was sure her parents didn't believe her. *Why could they not see it? What could she do to change their mind?*

As the evening wore on, things became more and more stressed. "*Mamm*, I heard the man say how easy it was. If you had seen the look on his face, you would know that I was telling the truth. He is a stone-cold killer, and we all know what Simon Glick is like."

"Stop this," Anna said. "If what you say is true, then you are putting yourself in grave danger. If this man really has killed Marlin Kanagy, then what is to stop him from killing you?"

Hope knew that this was true. It even churned her stomach and chilled her blood, but it didn't matter. What was right was right, and *gut* people stood up for truth and justice. If she backed down simply because she was afraid, then what did that make her? Certainly not a *gut* friend. Certainly not a *gut* Christian. Unfortunately, she had said this to her *mamm,* and it had not gone down well.

"We have to stand up for what is right, and if you won't do that, what does that make you? What sort of person are you?" Hope asked and instantly regretted her angry words.

"It makes me your *mamm*. I care more about you than Andy. I know you hate me for it, but one day you will understand."

"But he was once part of this family. Would you drop me as quickly?"

"Do not be silly. Leave this to the police. They know what they're doing, and you don't. You are behaving like a silly girl."

"Silly, believing in justice. Not wanting a killer to go free! I will find the truth *nee* matter what."

"You will not. I will ban you from leaving the *haus* if you continue this madness," Anna said.

Hope was sitting on the settee with her arm around the dog. She could feel him shivering a little at the raised tone of their voices, and she wanted to tell her *mamm* to stop it. To say that it was wrong to scare the animal. However, she sympathized with her *mamm,* and if she could've kept control of her anger, she would not have said the things she did. A touch of shame tempered her fury, but she would not back down. Andy had to be helped.

"Enough is enough," Samuel said. "Neither of you means the things you are saying, and neither off you want to see the wrong man convicted. However, Hope, this is dangerous. I do not want you to get involved. What you can do in the morning is go to see Emma King.

If she can draw the person you saw, then you will give that to the bishop. He will be the one who asks people if they know him. Do you understand?"

Hope nodded. She could accept this... it was a start.

"*Gut.* Both of us care about Andy. We always did. However, when someone suffers a loss like he did, they can go off the rails. If he didn't beat that man, then who did, and why didn't he tell us?"

Hope couldn't answer that question. *Had she been fooled by him? Was the sheriff right? Had a few sweet words kept her believing in her friend?* But, *nee*, she knew Andy. He couldn't have done this, and he definitely couldn't commit murder.

The atmosphere relaxed, and her *mamm* smiled and nodded. "Why don't I make us some cocoa and bring you a cookie before bed?" Anna asked.

"*Denke, Mamm,* that would be nice."

As they drank the cocoa and munched on the cookies, Hope wondered if she would be able to stay out of this. Maybe, she could just ask around a little. There would be no harm in it, would there?"

CHAPTER NINETEEN

* * *

Jesus said to her, "I am the resurrection and the life.
He who believes in me will live, even though he dies;
John 11:25

* * *

Hope made the dog a bed out of an old quilt in the corner of her room. Though he had not been too impressed with being bathed, he seemed to be settling into the home. After her prayers, she climbed into bed and tried to make a plan. Tomorrow, she would go and see Emma, and she spent the next few minutes trying to remember what the man looked like. It was difficult.

There was a little moonlight coming through the curtains, and she found herself staring up at the ceiling and letting out a sigh of frustration. Almost instantly, she felt a cold nose touching her arm. "You are such a *gut* boy, and you give me such comfort."

She patted the quilt on the bed beside her, and after a moment's hesitation, Truth jumped up. Walking around in a circle, he curled up beside her, his nose gently touching her leg. Though she doubted she would sleep, she, in fact, drifted straight away and didn't wake up until dawn.

Hope wanted to go straight to see Emma Byler, but her parents insisted she wait and have some breakfast.

"You can hardly turn up at the crack of dawn," her *mamm* said as she served a slice of breakfast casserole onto a plate.

The casserole smelled wonderful. It was made of eggs, sausage, cheese, and spinach and had always been one of her favorites. However, when she first looked at it, she just didn't fancy it. Truth touched her leg with his nose, and she looked down into big brown eyes. They were ever hopeful that they might get some of the casserole. "You've already had yours," she said.

"I think he's going to end up a bottomless pit," her *daed* said. "Don't you worry, boy; I will soon feed you up."

The dog trotted around the table and allowed Samuel to stroke him.

"Well, there was a tiny bit left," Anna said. "It's hardly enough to make a portion." Then, shrugging her shoulders, she tipped it into the dog's dish.

Truth raced over and wolfed it down before she even got back to the table. Then he sat and looked at them. It was almost as if he had a big smile on his face.

It seemed like he had made himself at home with all the family.

After breakfast, her parents went to the bakery, and Hope put Truth on the lead to go and visit Emma. For now, she was not going to let him off. The last thing she wanted was for him to run away. Did he have a home? What if someone was waiting for him or searching for him? *Nee*, somehow she didn't believe it. He was hers, he had been sent to her at the right time, at the time she needed him.

Truth was *gut* company as they made their way down the lane to Emma and Jesse King's *haus*. When she got there, she could see Emma sitting at an easel at the back of the property, looking out across the fields. The woman was around the same age as her *mamm* and had always been a little on the plump side. There were rumors that she had once been teased about it, as she had been teased about her paintings. Now, she was renowned in the local area and across the whole of the country. Her paintings were famous and demanded huge sums of money. Emma, however, or so her *mamm* told her, was exactly the same and gave much of her money to the district funds.

Hope froze. Could she ask this favor, and would it come to anything? For a moment, she thought about walking away. Perhaps everyone was right, and she should leave this alone. She knew that Andy would not want her to be in danger. But, *nee*, he didn't deserve to be locked up, and she had to know the truth. She cleared her throat and saw Emma look around.

"*Gut* day, Hope. How are you doing, and what can I do for you?" Emma asked, standing up from her easel.

The first thing Hope noticed was that she had a pretty face and a broad smile. The second thing was that her apron was patched with paint. Emma rubbed her hands on it as if to prove this point, transferring more blue onto the white apron.

"I wanted to ask you a favor," Hope said.

Emma looked down at Truth. "What a pretty-looking dog. Is he yours?"

"*Jah*, I found him in a snare, and he didn't wear a collar or anything, so... he... kind of became mine."

"That sounds like a *gut* thing. Lucky for him and maybe for you." She raised an eyebrow and smiled once more. "Come on inside. We will have a *kaffe* and talk about this. My eyes are getting tired. I could do with a break."

Emma led her into the kitchen. It was exactly the opposite of her Aunt Katie's. Though it was still big, with beautiful and sturdy kitchen units and a large oak table and chairs, it was cluttered with pots of paint, easels, and drying artwork.

"Sorry about the mess," Emma said. "Come in and take a seat. Bring the dog, I'm sure he'll like a cookie."

Hope settled herself at the table while Emma poured the *kaffe* and brought them some cookies. She threw one to Truth, who settled on the mat next to the door. "Now, what was that favor you wanted?" Emma asked as she sat down.

Hope quickly explained as much as she could. "I didn't see him that well, but I wondered if you could draw him from my description?"

"Hmmm, it's not something I've done before, but it's worth a try. I find the idea quite intriguing. Wait here while I grab a pad and pencil."

Emma was gone before Hope could even say *denke* and back almost as quickly.

"Now, tell me what he looked like?"

Hope froze. How did you describe someone? Could she remember, and what if she got it wrong and got the wrong person in trouble?

Despair went through her. Emma was willing to help, and yet she had failed. She had failed Andy, and she couldn't forgive herself. Tears streamed down her face, and she wanted to run. But, instead, she bit them back and looked up at Emma. "I'm sorry, I can't think what he looked like!"

CHAPTER TWENTY

* * *

*6 So then, just as you received Christ Jesus as Lord,
continue to live in him, 7 rooted and built up in him,
strengthened in the faith as you were taught,
and overflowing with thankfulness.*
Colossians 2:6-7

* * *

Hope fought back the tears and the despair of letting Andy down. She would just have to think of another way to help him. Only she couldn't. She felt a gentle hand on her own and looked up into Emma's pale blue eyes.

"Do not worry. You will remember a lot more than you think. Now, let me talk you through it."

Emma swallowed. Was there a chance that this could work? She nodded and wiped away her tears. As she did, she felt the dog lean against her and put her hand down to stroke his now soft and silky head.

"Okay, that's much better," Emma said. She was holding a pad of paper and a pencil. "Close your eyes and take three deep breaths. Do it with me. Breathe in slowly counting, one, two, three, four. Breathe out, let any tension go, one, two, three, four. Again, breathe in one, two, three, four. Breathe out, one, two, three, four. One last time, breathe in one, two, three, four. Breathe out, one, two, three, four. Now, keep your eyes closed and remember back to that day. You are in the woodland, you can hear people talking. You are looking out from behind a tree. What do you see?"

Hope found that the breathing steadied her, and she could almost feel the forest floor beneath her feet. Could feel the touch of wind on her cheek. She could see them, and she felt afraid just for a moment. But, *nee*, she was safe. So, she explained what she saw, and gently Emma took her through it until she was closer, and they came to that final moment when the man had turned just before he left.

"Freeze there and describe him for me," Emma said. "Start with just an overall picture, and we will go from there."

"Okay, I can see him. He was short, a good 6 inches shorter than Simon. He has one of those wiry builds that, at first glance, looks weak. However, it often means that the person is strong and quick. He has wispy brown hair about two inches long, and it falls over his face at times as it is lifted by the wind. His eyes are mean. They look dark, but it is too far to see the color. They are enough to make me fear him. That is all I can remember."

"What was he wearing?"

"Blue jeans, work boots, and a hooded sweatshirt. It was gray and looked worn. The hood wasn't up. I can't think of anything else. This is so generic it could be anybody."

"Don't worry, you are doing really, really well. I'm sure we can get somewhere from this," Emma said. "Now, open your eyes and have another cookie and a drink of *kaffe* while I finish off the overall drawing of him. Then we'll work on his face. For now, put it out of your mind and don't think of it."

Hope tried to do as she was told. She opened her eyes, sipped on the *kaffe*, and nibbled on another cookie. However, it was tasteless in her mouth, and she ended up passing most of it down to Truth. Though she thought she did it quite surreptitiously, she was sure that Emma knew. After what seemed like forever, but from the clock on the wall, it was only about six minutes, Emma put down her pencil and turned the page to show her.

Hope felt her mouth drop open. It was only a pencil drawing, and yet somehow Emma had captured the feel of what was going on in the woods and of the man she had seen. That drawing came to life in her mind, and she almost fell off her chair as she tried to jump backward.

"I'll take it from your reaction that this is pretty accurate," Emma said.

Hope nodded. She didn't trust her voice enough to speak.

"*Gut*, now let's work on the face. Once again, close your eyes and take in three deep breaths." She talked hope through her breathing and then asked her to think about what she had seen.

"In relation to his body, was his head large or small?"

Hope didn't understand the question and shook her head.

"I understand," Emma said. "Think about... in your family... think about your *daed*. He's a big man with a head that is in proportion to his body. Now, think about Amos Lapp. The two men are about the same size, but Amos's head is much bigger than Samuel's."

Hope couldn't help it, but she found herself chuckling. "I see, I see what you mean."

"Now, think about your Uncle Eli. He is of a slight build, not wiry like this man, but he has quite a large head. Maybe, to hold that big brain of his. Do you see what I mean?" She chuckled.

Hope did, but she thought the man's head had been about the right size. "I'm sorry, I think it was just a normal head."

"Okay, what shape was the face, long and thin, round, oval, or something else?"

Hope strained her memory, concentrating hard, and gradually an image appeared in her mind. She did remember the man had a long face and quite a big nose. With encouragement, Emma managed to tease lots and lots of detail that Hope didn't even know she'd seen, let alone remembered. Finally, after two hours, the drawing was finished, and Emma showed it to her. Before she did, she said, "If this is not right, then we can adjust it from here."

Hope held her breath as Emma turned the page to her. It was the man she had seen, even down to the evil glint in his mean eyes. "It's him."

After she left Emma's, Hope's intention was to rush straight to the bishop and let him take it from there. However, as she walked along the lane, she met people, and so she showed them the picture. But, unfortunately, *nee* one seemed to know who it was. One or two paused and thought about it, but *nee* one gave her an answer. With each negative response, she had a feeling of despondency, weighing heavier and heavier on her shoulders. Had this all been for nothing?

Then she came across Matilda Stoltzfus. Surely, Matilda might know who this was.

"Hope, it is so *gut* to see you," Matilda said. "We are all so relieved that Andy has been arrested. It frightens me so much that you might have married him and been hurt yourself."

Hope felt as if her legs would give way beneath her. Was this what people thought? Matilda was a friend and a *gut* friend of her parents. How could she think this way?

"New information has come to light," Hope said, swallowing down the bile of her anger. "It wasn't Andy who killed Kanagy, but this man. Do you know who he is?"

Matilda looked at the sheet of paper for a few long moments and then shook her head. "*Nee*, I don't recognize him. But, look, I'm sorry that many of us are pleased that this happened now and not a few years in the future. I know you are hurting, but you will get over him. I have to run, but if you need anything, come see me."

Hope's energy seeped from her as Matilda walked away. Tears were pushing at her eyelids. Truth bumped her leg, and she reached down and stroked him between the eyes.

"*Denke.*" Looking down at the dog's big brown eyes made her feel like she could face the world. "It is as if you know when I'm feeling down," she said.

Truth sat in the lane, his furry tail waved behind him, and his tongue stuck out. Even one day after she found him, he looked so much different. So much healthier. "Come on then, let's go see Bishop Amos," she said.

CHAPTER TWENTY-ONE

* * *

15 Let the peace of Christ rule in your hearts,
since as members of one body you were called to peace.
And be thankful.
Colossians 3:15

Hope made her way to the bishop's *haus*. As she got closer, she wondered if the bishop and Sarah would give her the same advice. Would they tell her she had dodged a bullet and that Andy was where he belonged?

"Hope, come on in. It is lovely to see you," Sarah, the bishop's *fraa,* said as she opened the door with a big smile. "Amos is working on his sermon. He will be glad of a break. I will show you through and then bring you both some *kaffe* and cake. I have a carrot cake that has just been iced."

Hope looked down at the dog and then back at Sarah. "I... can I... I don't want to leave him outside." The fear of the dog running away was too much for her. He was her comfort and strength.

"Of course, Amos told me all about the little fellow. Truth is it?" Sarah bent down and scratched the dog behind his ears. "What a wonderful name. Bring him, and I will get him a cookie as well."

She guided Hope through the kitchen and into the dining room. Amos lifted his head. His eyes looked a little weary, but a smile soon crossed his lips. Standing, he walked across and welcomed her into the room. "It is *gut* to see you and very timely. I have an appointment with the sheriff later today. Take a seat."

Almost as soon as Hope sat down, Sarah returned with the refreshments.

Hope sipped on her *kaffe* and tried to keep control of her excitement. "This meeting, is Andy coming home?"

Amos shook his head. "*Nee, nee,* I am sorry to get your hopes up. I just wanted to discuss a few things with the sheriff. To see how it is all going."

The disappointment was like a weight on her shoulders, but she had to keep hope; after all, it was her name. "I understand, but I have something that might help. She showed him the picture. "This is the man I saw taking the money from Simon Glick." She studied Amos's face as she pushed it across the polished wooden table. Maybe, he would recognize the man, and this would all be over. Only he didn't.

"This drawing is very realistic," Amos said. "I will take it to the sheriff and have some copies made. If we can find this man... it might help, but I don't want to get your hopes up too high."

Amos rubbed a hand through his hair and tugged on his long grey beard. He looked unsure; she had never seen him that way. In fact, he looked unsure and weary. How she hated to put this pressure on him; after all, he was very old.

"I understand," she said. "I can be patient as long as Andy realizes we have not forgotten him."

"He does. I have already written to him, and if you wish, I can send a letter from you."

That made her feel so much better, so she nodded. Amos handed her some paper and a pen, and she began to write a quick note. All she put was that she couldn't wait to see him again and that she believed he was innocent. She wanted to put in so much more, but she couldn't. This was enough, surely?

"As soon as you know anything, will you let me know?" she asked.

"Of course, I will. You have to understand, though, it might be weeks, even months." He was staring at her, willing her to understand. "That does not mean that I have forgotten him or that I have given up on him." This time he stared at her, and his eyes were harder. "I want you to promise me that you will not investigate this on your own. Whoever killed Marlin Kanagy is dangerous, and I do not want you to get hurt. That would help *nee* one. Do you understand me?"

Hope nodded, but he didn't release her from his stare. "*Jah*, I understand, and I won't do anything, I promise."

* * *

Amos had booked a driver to take him into Bird-in-Hand, but he expected the sheriff would return with him. Or at least he hoped he would. But, unfortunately, Buckner was not the best sheriff they had had. His father had been much more open and understood them much better.

The drive was quick, but as always, the car made him feel a little dizzy. When he got there, he had to stand for a moment before he went inside.

"Bishop, do you want me to wait for you?" John, the driver, asked.

"*Nee*, I can get a lift back, and if I do need you, I will call. Thank you, as always."

Amos made his way into the sheriff's station and across to Buckner's office. The man was working at his desk and looked up. Did annoyance cross his face? Amos thought it maybe did, but he pushed the thought from his mind. For now, he wanted this man's cooperation, and to get that, he would treat the man with respect and dignity and hope that it would be returned.

The sheriff stood and shook Amos's hand before pointing to a chair. "What can I do for you, Amos?"

"A couple of things, if that is okay. First, I'd like to know how the investigation to find Marlin Kanagy's murderer is going. The second, I have a drawing of the man that a witness thinks is the killer."

The sheriff pushed his chair away from the desk and leaned back before folding his arms and shaking his head. "Amos, we already have the killer, and I have enough evidence to get a conviction. So, why would I do any more work?"

Amos smiled what he hoped was a disarming smile. "Because you are a good man, and you want to make sure that the right person goes to jail."

"I already am sure. Now, if there's nothing else I can do for you?" He stood up.

Amos didn't. Instead, he pushed the drawing across the desk.

"What is this?" the sheriff asked, retaking his seat but refusing to look at the drawing.

"This is the man that Hope Miller saw in the woods. First, she heard a conversation with him that made her think he had been hired to kill Marlin. Then, she saw him accept a package of what she thinks is money. I do not think it would hurt to find this man and question him."

The sheriff kept his eyes fixed on Amos as the seconds ticked by. He was expecting Amos to stand and leave. It was a passive-aggressive movement and one that the bishop could easily withstand. Eventually, the sheriff shook his head and looked down at the drawing. There was no mistaking the flash of recognition that crossed his face. He knew this man, and he knew that he was bad news.

CHAPTER TWENTY-TWO

* * *

Peace I leave with you; my peace I give you.
I do not give to you as the world gives.
Do not let your hearts be troubled and do not be afraid.
John 14:27

* * *

Hope sat in her room. Right now, she just couldn't think of working on her soap, she had walked the dog, bathed and dressed his leg, fed and groomed him, and now she was stuck. All she could think about was Andy and Simon and the injustice that was ongoing. On her chest of drawers was another copy of Emma's drawing. This was the original one, and it was not quite as *gut* as the second one. There were a few erase marks and faint lines where Emma had changed what she was doing. Once she got it perfect, she made a second drawing.

Hope couldn't stop staring at it. It was as if the drawing was calling out to her and telling her to do something. Truth whined and touched her leg with his nose. She scratched him behind the ears, and he grumbled in pleasure.

"You're supposed to be resting," she said to him.

As if in response, he spun around, chasing his tail, and when he stopped, he barked at her.

It was *gut* to see him so happy and full of life. Just yesterday, he had looked like he wouldn't make it. "Well, I suppose we could go outside and enjoy some sunshine and maybe see a few people coming into the bakery. Perhaps, we could ask them about the picture?"

Truth barked again. It was almost as if he was agreeing with her. For a moment, Hope hesitated; she had made Amos a promise. Indecision swirled in her gut, making her stomach ache. *What should she do? Keep the promise or help Andy?* It didn't matter; she couldn't stop herself from helping.

So she nipped into the bakery and got a *kaffe* and one of the raspberry and white chocolate cookies she loved so much. With a couple of dog biscuits tucked into her apron, she took the drink and cookie and sat at the front of the bakery. The table closest to the entrance was empty, so she placed herself on it and put the picture in clear view closest to the walkway. Was she doing the wrong thing? What if the killer saw her or word got back to him?

She pushed the thoughts aside; she had to help Andy.

A car pulled into the bakery parking lot, and a young woman climbed out. She was staring a little bit. Obviously, this was her first time. It was something that they were used to. The bakery was famous not only among the Amish but also among the *Englischers*. There were many who came every week, but there were also what they called Lookey-Loos and first-timers.

"Can I ask a question?" Hope asked as the wide-eyed woman in the smart beige business suit drew level with her.

The woman looked at her and smiled. "Of course."

Hope got the feeling that this had probably made her day. "Do you recognize this man?"

She shook her head and looked bitterly disappointed. "No, I'm sorry, I don't. It's my first time here, but I've heard such good things about your strawberry tart. I hope they still have some left. My mother-in-law is coming, and I want to impress her."

"I'm sure they will have some left. Tell them that Hope Miller recommended it to you, that you are her friend."

"Thank you, I will, and have a lovely day."

Hope showed the picture again and again. *Nee* one seemed to know the man, and most people just wanted to tell her how lucky she was that Andy had been arrested. How they knew it was going to happen. How they tried to tell her to get away from him. Within about an hour, she was ready to pull off her *kapp*, stamp on it, and rip out her hair. Why couldn't they listen?

"I knew he was a bad one," Susan King said. She screwed up her face as if she had smelt something awful. "I wanted to tell you, I wanted to have him removed from the district. He should've been shunned. But, at least you are safe now that that evil man is locked up."

Hope stood and pushed back her chair. Tears were streaming down her face, for she could not take it any longer. "Why won't you listen to me? It wasn't him, but this man who killed Marlin, and he was paid by Simon Glick." Before the woman could pick her jaw off her chest, Hope turned and ran, and Truth came with her.

"What was that all about?" Simon Glick asked as he walked up behind Susan. "I thought I heard my name."

Susan shook her head. "Poor Hope, she is in love, and it makes you do strange things. She seems to think that you hired this man to kill Marlin. I've never heard anything quite so ridiculous in all my life."

"Let me look at that!" He pulled the picture from her hand and stormed away.

"I want to thank you for coming with me," Amos said to the sheriff as he drove his cruiser to the Glick farm.

"Whatever you may think about me, I do care about the law," the sheriff said.

"I don't doubt that," Amos said. "Turn into this driveway, here."

"This looks like quite a nice place." The sheriff let out a whistle as they drove between the white wooden fencing of the paddocks filled with fine horses and up to the large and impressive-looking double-fronted house.

"The Glick's are probably the richest family in Faith's Creek."

By the time the cruiser came to a stop, Jacob Glick had appeared at the door. He walked down to join them. "Bishop Amos, to what do I owe this pleasure?"

Jacob's face was lined, and he looked a *gut* 10 years older than he was. Clearly, he was worried, but he put a smile on his face. "Sheriff."

"We would like to talk to your son," Amos said. He noted the tension the statement caused in Jacob's jaw.

"Of course. Does he need a lawyer?"

"No, we just need to ask him some questions," the sheriff said. "We're actually looking for someone else that he might know."

Palatable relief crossed Jacob's face, and he seemed to stand a little taller. He may love his son, but it was clear that he expected the boy to cause trouble. "He's in the kitchen, having a sandwich and a piece of pie. Why don't you join us?"

They followed Jacob through the large entrance into a grand foyer with a double staircase in front of them. They crossed the polished wooden floor and went through a door into the kitchen that would fit half of Amos's *haus* and still have room for a party. There was a large island in the middle, and to one side, the table that looked like it could seat 16. Simon was sitting on the far side, munching on what looked like a cherry pie.

"What's all this?" he said through a mouthful of food.

"Didn't I teach you to close your mouth and swallow before speaking," Jacob said, shaking his head. "The sheriff and the Bishop are looking for someone. They just want your help. So I suggest you cooperate." Jacob turned back to Amos. "My *fraa's* away visiting her family. Can I get you anything?"

"*Nee, denke*, we will take it from here," Amos said, and they approached the table.

Simon was finding it hard to sit still. His eyes were looking anywhere but at the bishop and the sheriff.

The sheriff slapped the picture down on the table. "Who is this man?" He asked.

"Why d'ya want to know?" Simon kept his eyes away from the picture; a drip of sweat ran off his brow and dropped onto the table.

"He is wanted in connection with a robbery. A witness said they saw him in this area and that you might have been seen with him."

Simon's face turned white, and he looked down at the picture. Recognition opened his mouth. A piece of cherry pie dropped out; he closed it quickly and looked up. "It wasn't me."

"Well, we need to find him. It could be urgent," Amos said. They had discussed this on the way over and decided they wouldn't tell him why they were looking for the man. Or that they knew his name was Brad Henderson.

"We have reason to believe that he killed Marlin Kanagy," the sheriff said.

Amos was surprised at the sheriff. That wasn't what they had intended to do, but as he watched the emotions cross Simon's face, he realized that the sheriff was being quite canny. Simon had gone into a complete panic.

"Well, Brad Henderson is gone!" The look on Simon's face was one of superiority. He thought he had them.

"And because you can't find him, you can't prove anything." Simon pushed back from the table and almost ran from the room.

CHAPTER TWENTY-THREE

10 So do not fear, for I am with you;
do not be dismayed, for I am your God.
I will strengthen you and help you;
I will uphold you with my righteous right hand.
Isaiah 41:10

* * *

"Well, that was informative," the sheriff said. "The fool admitted he knew the man."

Amos pushed his chair back. He felt weary. *How had he allowed this to happen? Why hadn't he spoken to Simon sooner?* For a moment, he wondered if it was time for him to step down.

"Don't look so worried, Amos."

"I will fetch him back." Amos began to rise.

The sheriff shook his head, stood up, and picked his hat off the table. "There is nothing we can do until we find Brad."

"Then we must force Simon to tell us where he is."

The sheriff's eyes widened. "Amos, I'm ashamed of you. I can't force the young man. I follow the law. I don't know what you do out here, but I will have none of it."

Amos sighed. The look on the sheriff's face was one of disgust. "I meant by talking to him. By showing him it is the right thing to do and getting his father to do so too."

"I don't think that will work; come with me." The sheriff didn't wait for Amos to answer but simply walked out of the *haus*.

Amos found his knees aching as he stood and his back throbbing. All he wanted to do was go home and sit next to the fire, but he would see this through. Andy was a *gut* man; of that, he was sure. He would make sure that his reputation was restored if it was the last thing he did.

He found the sheriff talking to Jacob next to the cruiser. It was clear that Jacob recognized the man in the drawing. Jacob was not happy about it either, but it seemed he didn't know where he was. The sheriff tipped his hat to Jacob and climbed into the cruiser.

"I'm sorry," Jacob called. "I will help in any way I can."

Amos nodded to him and climbed into the cruiser. *Why did these things have to be so low?*

"I feel like we are letting Andy down," Amos said.

"Don't. I'm starting to believe you."

"But you said...."

"I did. Until we find Brad, there is little I can do... but I think I have an idea. Also, Jacob said that his son was angry and muttering about Hope Miller. I guess she didn't stay home, and he has seen she has the picture."

Amos felt a jolt of pain in his chest. Had they put Hope in danger? "We must go and protect her."

"No, we are going to park up at the edge of the woods and watch to see where that boy goes. Then we are going to follow him." The sheriff looked Amos up and down. "Are you well enough for this? I don't want to injure you."

Amos got the feeling that the sheriff was more worried that he would slow him down, but he wouldn't. "I may be old and a little creaky, but I will follow you wherever needed to save an innocent man."

"That's the spirit. Quick, he's watching us, and I don't want to spook him." The sheriff started the engine, and Amos jumped when it roared into life. He should have been used to such things by now. He had ridden in them maybe 50 times in his life; perhaps his nerves were just on edge today.

Why did people hate Andy so much? Hope could no longer hold back her tears, so she turned and ran, taking Truth with her. Pressure and failure drove her forward. All she wanted to do was escape the looks and plati-tudes. It all seemed so unfair, and she tore across the fields until she was under cover of the trees. They hid her from accusing looks and wrapped their comforting branches around her. Still, she ran on, hoping she would find some peace here. Maybe, she would even discover an answer. A way to free Andy.

Her feet were nimble as she sprinted across the woods, going deeper and deeper and not even noting where she was. At last, she had finally outrun her emotions. Exhausted, she dropped to the ground in a pile of leaves. Truth jumped onto her lap and licked the tears from her cheeks. "I'm so lucky to have you." She hugged the little dog close and wondered at how gracious he was after all he had been through.

It was peaceful here. There was nothing but the sound of the leaves caressed by the wind and the occasional bird song. Truth was panting, but it didn't last long, and he curled up on her lap, nestled in her skirt.

Hope closed her eyes and whispered a prayer as she stroked his silky fur. In her prayer, she asked for the strength to stand by Andy and the wisdom to help him. She also asked that people would see the truth and understand that he was not a bad man.

Opening her eyes, she looked around and wondered where they were. Her long run through the woods had taken them off the beaten track, and she didn't recognize anything. She also couldn't remember which way she had come from. How could she be so silly?

Looking around, her bare feet had left no trail, and a feeling of worry wormed its way inside of her. What should she do?

"Truth, can you find a way out of here?"

The little dog tilted its honey-colored head and looked at her quizzically.

Hope chuckled. "You have *nee* idea, do you?" It was no *gut*. She had to start walking somewhere. Looking up, the sun was directly overhead. That gave her *nee* help. However, she knew that Faith's Creek was east of the forest. No matter what happened, she would not stay lost for long.

After a quick look around, she decided to head off in one direction. It was as *gut* as any other, and she had a feeling that pulled her that way.

Truth was happy. The dog had eaten well and loved to be out. To him, this was just an adventure. But as the minutes passed by, and nothing familiar could be seen, Hope was filled with trepidation. *Where was she going?*

Then she saw a track ahead and ran to it. It was not one she recognized, but it was a track which meant it had to lead somewhere. So, she turned right and followed it for another 15 minutes when they came out of the trees into a clearing. Truth pulled back and began to shiver. She looked down at him and noticed his hackles were raised, and he was almost cowering.

"What is it, boy?"

The dog looked as if it was going to run away. *What had she stumbled onto?*

CHAPTER TWENTY-FOUR

* * *

6 Do not be anxious about anything,
but in every situation,
by prayer and petition,
with thanksgiving,
present your requests to God.
7 And the peace of God,
which transcends all understanding,
will guard your hearts and your minds in Christ Jesus.
Philippians 4:6-7

* * *

Hope had always been told that if she was alone in the woods and something spooked her, that she should not instantly run away. That she should assess the situation first. It was difficult to follow that advice. Every instinct told her to run, but she stopped herself. The basic principle was that an animal might chase you if you ran. Not that she was scared of any animal, the threat she faced was much more malicious than that. However, running in a panic through the forest was a recipe for disaster.

Today had not been a *gut* day, her emotions were all over the place, and she needed to know what the dog was scared of. Maybe, she would find the awful people who had mistreated him. If she did, they would be getting a lashing from her tongue. But, her greater worry was that she would find the killer. What would she do then?

Indecision caused her to hesitate. Instinct told her to go in the opposite direction, to listen to Truth. But her heart, it wanted her to go forward. If there was any chance of helping Andy, she had to take it, *nee* matter the risk to herself.

Even though she was afraid, her anger gave her a touch of courage. She reached down and stroked the dog. At first, he was shivering, but he relaxed under her touch and looked up at her with trusting eyes.

"We're just going to go a little further," she said and began to walk along the lane. It curled around to the right. As she walked, more of the clearing came into view, along with a cabin.

Where was this? How far was she from Faith's Creek? Though she thought she knew the area well, she didn't know this place existed, until now. *Should she go any further, or should she go back and fetch help? What would she tell them? I found a cabin in the woods, and it scared me?*

Though her brain wanted her to turn and run from there, her heart wanted her to go a little further. Why!? What did she expect to find?

Truth was shivering once more. She could feel him shaking against her leg. It was clear that he did not want to be here. "Just a little further," she said, stroking him gently. He leaned into her hand and relaxed.

Skirting along the edge of the trees, she moved to the front of the cabin. Sitting on the steps was the man from the drawing.

Fear froze her blood and fixed her to the spot.

She was only frozen for moments, but it seemed like forever. She could not breathe and could not move. *Was this the man who killed Marlin Kanagy? Was this the proof she needed to free Andy?*

Truth leaned against her leg, which was enough to bring her out of her stupor. She turned, but as she did, she stood on a dried stick. It snapped, echoing through the woods, and she moaned as it dug into her foot.

"Hey, you, what are you doing here?" the man called.

Hope turned back to see him rise to his feet and start toward her. Terror raised the hairs on her arms and sent oxygen to her heart and blood vessels. With the dog pulling on the lead in fear, she raced away as quickly as her legs would carry her. *But where would she run to, and could she outpace him?*

Amos and the sheriff followed Simon into the woodlands but kept their distance. Even so, the young man was paranoid and maybe had a second sense, for he kept looking around and almost spotting them.

"We need to drop back a little," the sheriff said.

"I don't want to lose him," Amos said. "I'm worried about Hope."

"I'm pretty sure she's not out here in the woodland," the sheriff whispered, "now, follow my lead."

Amos did as he was told and waited while the distance between them and Simon increased. He knew the area better than the sheriff but had *nee* idea where Simon was going. The man wasn't following a path and, at times, seemed to be walking in circles. *Was he just angry? Or did he have a purpose?*

Amos had been looking down at his feet to make sure that he didn't break branches or stumble, and when he looked up, he almost bumped into the sheriff's back.

"What is it?" Amos asked.

The sheriff shrugged and turned to him. "I'm sorry, I think I lost him. I guess we should go back, and I will put an APB out on Brad Henderson. We will have to wait for that."

Failure was like a heavy cloak on Amos's back. He didn't want to give in, not yet. "Do you have enough to release Andy?"

The sheriff shook his head. "No, we have nothing at the moment but a suspicion."

"Then, do you mind if we give this a little longer?" Amos asked. "I know these woods; let me lead."

The sheriff's eyes widened a little. It was clear that he didn't think Amos was capable of running around in the woods, let alone leading him. However, after a moment, he nodded.

Amos closed his eyes and whispered a prayer, allowing his senses and his spirituality to guide him. Maybe, *Gott* would be listening. Feeling a pull to his right, Amos turned in that direction. Now, he felt excited and infused, and his pace increased. He just hoped that it was in the right direction.

Hope was running so fast and constantly looking behind her that she didn't see the tree root until it was too late. Her foot caught in it, and she was sent crashing to the floor, dropping the leash. The fall knocked the wind from her; she hurt her elbow and let out a squeal on landing. Truth stopped for a moment and then looked as if he would bolt. She couldn't bear the thought of losing him and being here all alone, with her pursuer gaining ground. Pushing, she tried to stand, but a wave of dizziness sent her back to the ground, and she noticed blood dripping. Reaching up, she felt her head. There was a bump, and it was bleeding. She must have hit it in the fall.

The dog was unsure what to do. Looking from her to the safety of the trees and back again.

"Looks like I found you," Brad said from behind her.

Truth began to bark and rushed past her, racing at him with fury and frenzied barks. The wiry-looking man jerked backward, a look of fear on his face, but it didn't last long. He danced to one side and then kicked out his foot connecting with Truth's ribs and sending him up into the air.

Hope felt her heart break as the dog squealed, and she heard a thud as he hit the ground, and then nothing. "Truth, where are you?" She tried to get to her feet, but Brad was in front of her and pushed her back down.

"You did it, didn't you?" Hope shuffled back, her eyes searching the ground for Truth. Where was he?

"I've done a lot of things. What you blaming me for?"

"You murdered Marlin Kanagy, and I will see you go to jail for it."

He laughed. "Yeah, I did it for the old man, but you are going to be too dead to tell anyone about it."

"Why are you still here?" Simon shouted as he came out of the trees. "I told you to get out of here and keep a low profile."

"I have another job next week. After that, I'll be gone," Brad said, turning to face Simon.

Hope scuttled back. *Could she get away now? But what about Truth, could she leave him?*

Brad reached down and grabbed her ankle so fast that she didn't even see it. "You ain't going nowhere."

Hope realized that she had failed. Not only had she let Andy down, but she had let the dog down too. Now it seemed that she would die here alone in these woods.

CHAPTER TWENTY-FIVE

* * *

For the LORD watches over the way of the righteous,
but the way of the wicked leads to destruction.
Psalm 1:6

* * *

Hope kicked out at the hand that held her and thrashed as hard as she could. He tightened his fingers, digging into her ankle. It hurt, but she wriggled and kicked with all her might. At last, her ankle pulled free, and she struggled to her feet. Brad pulled back his fist, and she knew he was going to punch her, but Simon grabbed hold of his arm before he could. She heard them scuffle and began to race away through the woods. In her heart, she wanted to go back for Truth, but she couldn't. However, she would come back later. She wouldn't abandon him.

Her heart was in her throat, and her breathing was coming in great gasps, but she raced as fast as she could through the woodland. She could hear them squabbling behind her and arguing and hoped that this would keep them busy long enough for her to escape.

Where should she run? Which direction? She didn't have time to stop and get her bearings, so she just ran as fast and hard as possible.

"Come back and face the music," Brad shouted after her. "You ain't getting away."

Hope pushed on even faster, a fresh bout of fear boosting her adrenaline and making her legs work even harder. The brush seemed to be getting thicker. She hoped this meant that they were nearing the edge of the woodland when more light allowed more shrubs and bushes to grow. Then, hopefully, she would end up somewhere near Faith's Creek, and someone would help her. *But what if she came out in the middle of the fields?* There was no way she could run across the field faster than the two men. Her skirt restricted her movement, her ankle hurt, and her head throbbed from the fall. And she was shorter than Simon was. He would easily outpace her.

Tears streamed down her face; she wanted to help so many and didn't want to fail them or herself.

It was getting lighter, she was coming to the edge of the woodlands, and as she burst out into the sunshine, she was grabbed by strong hands and let out a squeal. One more burst of adrenaline and she hit out, only to stop.

Bishop Amos put a finger to his lips and pulled her into his arms. "There, you are fine, you are safe, we have got you," he whispered.

Moments later, Brad Henderson rushed through the trees straight into the sheriff's arm. He was knocked from his feet onto the grass. The sheriff had a knee in his back and his hands clasped behind him just as Simon came out of the woodland.

Simon was blinking as he took in what he saw. "Well, I chased him out for you," Simon said, standing tall and looking as pleased as punch.

The sheriff had, by this time, handcuffed Brad. He pulled out his gun and pointed it at Simon. "Get on your knees."

"But.. but... I came across this man and rescued Hope," Simon tried to convince them.

The sheriff took no notice, holstered his gun, and took out another set of handcuffs. He spun Simon around and slapped them on him. "Sorry, son, but it's over." He then read both of the men their rights.

"I have to go back and search for Truth," Hope said as the Bishop tried to steer her back toward home.

"I don't think you have to," the bishop said.

Tears were streaming down Hope's cheeks. "You don't understand. He helped me even though he was afraid, he helped me." The bishop spun her around and pointed.

Walking slowly and with a limp, Truth appeared out of the bushes. As soon as he saw Hope, his whole body began to wiggle, and he squirmed over to her. She dropped down and pulled him into her arms. "You are such a *gut* little dog, and I love you so much," Hope said as she kissed the dog's soft head.

The next few hours were a whirlwind of events. First, Hope was reunited with her parents, who had been blissfully unaware of the drama. Then, Doctor Yoder checked her over and attended to her wounds. The bump on her head was nasty but didn't require stitches.

Amos explained what had happened on *rumspringa*. That Simon, not Andy, had been the one who beat up the man. That Andy saved him but was caught at the scene, covered in blood and bruised by his interaction with Simon. Most of it had been his own blood where Simon had hit him. As is their tradition, he took the blame. Falsely thinking that he was being of service.

"Oh, Hope, we are so sorry," Anna said as she hugged Hope and stroked her back. "So sorry that we put you in danger and that we doubted Andy."

"*Mamm*, it is all right. I just want to see Andy and welcome him home."

"That is *gut*. Go have a shower; we will talk to the bishop."

Samuel hugged her before she took Truth back to the *haus* and ran a hot shower. "As for you, Truth," she said, giving him some cooked chicken breast. "You need to rest and heal. But, don't worry, you have a home here and in my heart."

Truth wolfed down the chicken and then went to a dog bed that had appeared in the kitchen. He curled up and was instantly asleep, looking very comfortable.

* * *

"Amos, when will Andy be released?" Anna asked once Hope was out of earshot.

"The sheriff says he can be released by tomorrow. It will probably be mid-afternoon before the paperwork can be completed. They will let him know tonight. The sheriff is going to collect Hope to meet him."

"That is wonderful," Anna said.

"We should have trusted him." Samuel was shaking his head and looking most distressed.

Anna took his hands. "It is our *boppli* girl, do not be hard on yourself."

"I know, but we knew him. We let him down."

"*Ack*, we did. We will make it up to him. How about a party tomorrow night?" Anna raised an eyebrow as she had the idea.

"That would be a wonderful idea." Samuel's face lit up, and he began to nod his head as ideas of what to do came through his mind. "How about we arrange a party here and have the sheriff bring him to it. That way, Andy will know that all of Faith's Creek welcomes him home?

"That is a wonderful idea. I will let people know," Amos said. "He will be exonerated, I promise you."

CHAPTER TWENTY-SIX

* * *

I have fought the good fight,
I have finished the race,
I have kept the faith.
2 Timothy 4:7

* * *

"Mamm, what is happening?" Hope asked as a wagon arrived with the service benches and tables the following afternoon. She had been on tenterhooks waiting for Andy to be released. It was taking too long, in her mind.

Anna smiled and pulled her into a hug. "We wanted this to be a surprise. We didn't want to tell you in case it didn't happen. Andy is coming home, and we are having a party to welcome him back."

Hope felt her heart fill with joy and her eyes with tears. Happy tears, this time. "*Denke*. Can I help?"

Anna nodded, too emotional to speak.

Before long, the *haus* was buzzing with conversations and expectations. Everyone had brought food, and the scent of fried chicken filled the air, as well as freshly baked bread. But Hope wasn't hungry. *Where was Andy? What was taking so long?*

"I'm so sorry for what I said," Susan King said as they passed in the kitchen. "I brought a shoofly pie, and if that boy wants anything, you tell him to come to me."

Hope nodded. Her emotions were boiling over. Part of her wanted to scream at people, and the rest of her wanted to hug them. *But where were the sheriff and Andy? Had something happened?*

As tears pressed against her eyelids, she raced up the stairs to her room. Inside, Truth was curled up on her bed. All these people had been too much for him. He was happier here, out of the way. He looked adorable and completely at home. She sat next to him, and he crawled onto her lap. Fighting back the tears, she stroked his coat. It was so springy and so smooth it felt like warmed silk. The act calmed her, and she began to pray, offering her gratitude for Andy's release.

As she whispered, "Amen," a vehicle pulled into the driveway. Kissing Truth, she left the room and raced down the stairs. The door opened, and Andy walked in. Hope couldn't help herself. She jumped into his arms. Andy picked her off the floor and spun her around. She clung on tight to him until she heard her *daed* clearing his throat.

Hope stepped back quickly and could see Andy grinning at her. "I hear you were the one who believed in me," he said.

"Always."

"*Denke.*"

Hope fought back her tears. "I have so much to tell you." But before she could say anymore, he was herded away by the crowd. People were patting him on the back and saying they believed in him.

"Hope, join me in the kitchen," Bishop Amos said.

Hope felt her stomach flip. Was she about to be told off for her inappropriate behavior? It didn't matter; she had been so pleased to see Andy and knew she would do it again.

Amos was pouring two mugs of *kaffe*, and he handed her one. "Drink this; it will help," he said.

"I'm sorry. I was so happy to see him."

"*Ack*, that doesn't matter." His eyes raised to her and widened a little. "This time; don't make a habit of it until you are married."

Hope shook her head as her cheeks burned with embarrassment. Married, what did he mean?

"I want both you and Andy to understand that if you need anything, you are to come and see me."

"We will, *denke*."

"*Gut*, let's grab some food and go and eat.

They walked back into the living room, which was filled with people. Andy was surrounded, and everyone was smiling. It filled Hope's heart with joy.

"I know that Glick boy was *nee gut*," Susan said.

Bishop Beiler cleared his throat loud enough to stop the conversation. "Has *nee* body learned a thing?! Judging is not your job; leave that to *Gott* and treat all as you wish to be treated."

As the conversation began to buzz around the room, Andy came over. "Can I talk to you?"

"Of course," Hope said.

"Before you do, what are your plans?" Amos asked.

Andy's face turned pale. "I don't know. I have *nee* where to live and *nee* job, but I will manage."

"I guess Old Man Kanagy never told you about his will." Amos smiled as Andy shook his head.

"I don't understand. Why would he have a will?" Andy asked.

"Marlin had a few problems with his health. He had confided in me," Amos said. "He asked me to keep it to myself, but he didn't have long. Nothing made him happier than being in that *haus* on the farm with you."

Hope felt a lump in her throat.

"*Denke*, that fills my heart, but I wish I could have saved him," Andy said with tears in his eyes.

"Well, he loved you like a son, and he left the *haus* and the farm to you. I know it will be bittersweet going back there but remember the *gut* times. That is what he would want."

"*Denke*, Amos, *denke* so much for believing in me."

Amos put a hand on his shoulder. "Always. I saw into your heart, and I know it is filled with *gut*. Now, go, take this one for a walk. I will cover for you." Amos winked as they left.

Hope led Andy out the back door and across the field to the creek. She had had enough of the woods for now. As they walked, their hands brushed together, setting butterflies swirling inside her.

For a few minutes, they walked in silence. There was nothing but the breeze and a pair of birds circling above them. Riding on the thermals and catching the setting sun. It was a magnificent sight and took Hope's breath away as the sky turned blue to orange.

Andy stopped in front of her and turned to face her. "I can never *denke* enough for what you did for me. I am so grateful, but never put yourself in danger for me."

"I just asked a few questions and ended up in the right place," she said.

"And you have a dog now. I can't wait to meet him."

"He is very cute and called Truth." She blushed again and lowered her head. Then an awful thought came to her. "Do you like dogs?"

"I love them."

Hope let out a sigh. "That is *gut*."

"Can I drive you to service?" he asked.

"*Jah*, I would love that... does that mean you want to court me?"

Andy stared at her for long moments, and she wondered if she had misread the signs. Perhaps this was just as friends. Disappointment washed over her, but he leaned forward and kissed her lips. A sweet gesture that made her gasp and reach out for him, but he had already pulled away.

"I don't want to court you...."

Hope's heart stopped, and disappointment filled her.

"I love you, and I want to marry you," Andy said, turning away. "I'm so sorry. I don't know where that came from. I promised myself that if I ever got out, that I would prove to you and your parents that I could look after you. Then

I would court you, and maybe in a year, I would ask if you would marry me. Forget I said that."

Hope smiled, his cheeks were glowing, and his head was bowed. With a finger under his chin, she lifted it up. Taking a step closer, she kissed him. "*Jah*, I would love to be your *fraa*. I love you too, silly."

Andy pulled her into his arms and kissed her once more, a deep kiss, before pulling away. "Bishop Amos will have my guts for garters if I don't take you back soon."

"It would be worth it," she said. "I love you so much."

"As I love you."

Hand in hand, they walked back to the party.

Amos winked at them when they came in. "I'm free tomorrow after 11 if you need to talk to me."

Hope knew that the smile on her face was the biggest she had ever worn. She was sure they would be visiting the bishop to tell him of their marriage tomorrow.

EPILOGUE

* * *

For I know the plans I have for you," declares the LORD,
"plans to prosper you and not to harm you,
plans to give you hope and a future.
Jeremiah 29:11

* * *

3 YEARS LATER

Hope Byler looked out the kitchen window at her *mamm* and *daed* playing with her son, Marlin Byler. It was his 1st birthday, and they were down on their hands and knees. Samuel was pretending to be a monster, and Anna had knitted a horse, cow, and a ball for him and was moving them around as if they were real.

Lying next to them was Truth. Every time the knitted ball rolled near him, his paw shot out to it. Which caused Marlin to chuckle and wave his little hands.

Hope had never been so happy.

"Why are you hiding in here?" Andy said as he came up behind her and kissed her ear.

"I was just enjoying watching everyone have such fun. How about you? Have you finished for the day?"

"*Jah*, I only had a bit of work to do. The men will do the rest."

Hope leaned back against his chest. They had two farm-workers now. The farm was growing, and everything was going so well. She still made her soap but was considering stopping it in the next 4 or 5 months. So far, she hadn't mentioned it to Andy, but she didn't think he would mind.

"Come," she said, taking his hand. She led him outside. As soon as he saw her, Truth ran over. "Hello, little man," she said, stooping down and stroking his head.

As she stood up, her hand went instinctively to her belly.

Anna was watching her with the keen eyes only a *mamm* could have. A smile came over her face, and she mouthed a question, "Are you?"

Hope blushed and nodded. The problem was she hadn't told Andy yet. Typical of her *mamm* to spot her secret first. She couldn't help but smile and realized that she had to tell Andy. It had only been confirmed earlier today, but she had suspected it for a few weeks.

"Just come inside with me for a moment," she whispered as they got to the table.

He let out a breath, for he was hungrily eyeing the fried chicken and boiled potatoes swimming in fresh butter. "Can it wait?"

"*Nee*, I need to tell you something."

He looked up at her, and concern filled his eyes. "Are you ill? The morning sickness has me worried!" His face changed, and he slapped his own forehead. His eyes were wide and questioning.

It seemed she would not get to tell him in private. She nodded.

Andy let out a whoop of joy and lifted her off her feet. Spinning her around while Truth barked with joy, and Marlin let out a peal of laughter.

"What is going on?" Samuel asked.

"Put me down, you oaf," Hope said. "I'm getting dizzy."

"Oh, sorry." Andy set her on her feet. His face was full of contrition, his eyes apologetic.

"Don't worry, I'm fine." She took his hand and faced her parents. "I'm going to have a *boppli*."

Her parents both stood up and let out cries of joy.

"When?" Anna asked as she came around to Hope.

Samuel was hugging Andy.

"In around 6 months," Hope said as they sat at the table. Truth was at her side as they talked, ate, and looked after *boppli* Marlin. Food and conversation flowed until the sun went down, painting the sky in orange, red, and then purple.

Once everyone had left and Marlin was asleep in his crib, Hope was looking out the kitchen window at the fields and the view down to the creek. The moon was bright, and she could see surprisingly well. Andy put his arms around her and leaned his chin on her shoulder. "I love you so much," he said.

"I love you too. I am so happy and so grateful for all we have,"

He spun her around and kissed her on the lips. "I love you so much and this little one. I love him or her already." He put his hand on her belly before dropping to his knees and kissing it.

He stood up, and Hope melted into his arms. It had taken Hope, faith, and courage to get where they were, but she was so happy and fulfilled. This was like a dream come true. For long moments she listened to his heartbeat and thanked *Gott* for all they had.

* * *

If you missed any of these much loved books, find all the series here or read on for a great value offer.

THE CHERISHED LOVE COLLECTION – 30 BOOK BOX SET – PREVIEW

"For I know the plans I have for you," declares the Lord,
"plans to prosper you and not to harm you,
plans to give you hope and a future."
- Jeremiah 29:11

* * *

It was the first time in the past year that any of them could breathe, really breathe. Zook... Rebecca hated it, almost as much as she hated Rebecca. Yet that didn't matter. It would be their new last name as Rebecca was her new first name.

Anger and fear fought for control as she thought of all she would miss. She had just turned 16, and now she had to leave it all behind, everything. Her friends, school, boys, parties, everything including her own name was gone. For a moment, she thought of her mom, kind eyes and a sweet smile filled her mind. They were so much alike, both tall and slim with honey blonde hair and blue eyes, but she would never see her again. How could that be? How could someone so filled with love be gone so quickly, so instantly and so horribly? The thoughts threatened to choke her, but she shook them away. It was too painful, even now. But that was not the worst of it.

"Maybe it will be fun," Eli said.

"Fun? You only think it's fun because you're a kid and you don't have any friends yet," Rebecca said mentally calling him Eli in her mind like the Marshal told them.

"Hey, I'm not a kid. I'm in double digits now, just like you. I can make my own decisions, and I can think for myself. I do think this will be fun. I think it'll be awesome, not just fun but awesome."

Even looking at her brother seemed to make her mad. Cody, no don't call him that even to yourself. The words of the Marshal rang in her ears and seemed to make her blood boil. It was so unfair. Eli, as her brother was now called, looked more like their dad, he would be strong and broad, and he had thick black hair that stood up at all different angles. Right now he looked stupid in his black pants, suspenders, and white shirt. Even the straw hat made her want to laugh. A cringe went through her as she remembered what she was wearing. *Could this get any worse?*

"Keep living in your little fantasy world, Eli. There's nothing awesome about this," Rebecca almost spat the words out. "I bet after a week of not playing your stupid little video games you're going to be balling your eyes out and begging to go back home. Begging to go back to our crappy little apartment in our crappy old city."

"Don't be so hard on your little brother, Rebecca. He's only ten. And besides, I think it could be fun."

"Really Dad? After everything that's happened, after everything you've done, after Mom, and now this, how you can say this could possibly be fun?"

Aaron took a deep breath, but he did it like an expert, one used to trying to hide the frustration and anger he was feeling. If only he could've done that when it really mattered, but what Rebecca said stung. It stung like the biggest, meanest yellow jacket he had ever seen when he was just a kid playing on a playground in his hometown. He remembered the venom that yellow jacket sunk into his arm. It was the worst feeling he could remember, but this was more punishing because it was all true.

"Well, I do think this it's a little cool, that we get to ride in a horse-drawn buggy with real horses," Rebecca's younger sister Lydia added.

"Oh, please. Haven't you noticed that smell? That's not air freshener you know. That's horse crap, just like our life, crap, and it keeps falling down on us every so often. I promise you, you're both going to hate this in a few weeks, probably sooner."

Lydia just sighed and put her head back into her journal. At thirteen, she didn't talk much and kept her nose in a book scribbling or writing at all times. It annoyed Rebecca because she thought they should stick together. After all, Lydia had lost her mother too. A lock of brown hair had escaped Lydia bonnet and furled on her cheek. Lydia was a strange mix of both parents. She had Dad's brown eyes and auburn hair that had blonde streaks in the sunshine. Once she had always been happy, but since their mom's death, she had been so withdrawn.

"Rebecca, just give it a chance," Dad's voice wavered, he hadn't even convinced himself. "This is our new life now. We have a real opportunity here if we just let ourselves see where it takes us. We need to learn to make the most of it."

"And why is that Dad? Why is that? Tell me? Why do we need this new godforsaken opportunity? You messed up, you always do. You're such a loser, Dad. You say you're so smart, but there's nothing smart about you. I don't see what Mom ever saw in you, and now she's dead. You killed her. You killed her!" Rebecca felt her voice rise as the pain took over. A vision of flying blood, of Mom falling and the explosive sound of a gunshot, filled her mind. Again she shook it away. Before it brought tears to her eyes. That sign of weakness, it would be too much to bear. No one could see her cry, not now, not ever.

"Hey, that's not fair. I didn't kill your Mom. I had no control over that bullet that came into our home," Aaron's voice trailed off as if he didn't believe it himself.

Sensing his weakness Rebecca pounced. "Don't give me that. You know good and well it's your fault. If you hadn't been doing what you were doing... Mom worked so hard, so hard to take care of us, to feed us, and what were you doing? Playing poker, playing the horses, playing all your stupid little games, just like Cody... oh sorry, Eli." Sarcasm burst out from her rant, he had it coming. Rebecca continued before he had a chance to defend himself. "ELI..." she yelled, "Eli didn't use our money. He didn't borrow someone else's money. He didn't go out and get drunk and do all those stupid things... but you did."

"Listen, I know I've made a lot of mistakes, but I...."

"Mistakes? Mistakes!" Rebecca repeated.

"I worked too. I had a job too. I wasn't just sitting at home watching television all the time," Aaron's voice almost pleaded.

Eli's head was down and he looked close to tears. Rebecca hated herself, but she couldn't seem to stop. The words had a life of their own and had to be said. They ripped out of her like a hurricane. For a second she wondered what damage they would cause, but still she couldn't stop them.

"Well, that would've been better. At least, if you didn't have a job and you were just a lazy bum, you wouldn't have gambled away the rest of Mom's money, but you did. Didn't you? You spent all the money from your sorry little part-time job."

"I did the best I could."

"The best you could? Really? You got fired from your last job because you came in drunk. You only had that job because of Mom's old boyfriend from high school. You've been a drunk as long as I can remember. Here's a thought. Why didn't you ever think to stop drinking and actually do something productive with your life?"

"Stop it. You're hurting my ears," Eli shouted as he put his hands over his ears.

"You are a little loud, Rebecca," Lydia added as she continued doodling on her tiny sketchbook to while away the long ride.

"A little loud? A little loud? How about this? Is this loud enough for you? You're a loser, Dad, a loser. I swear you killed her. You killed mom. Mom. It's your fault, but you should be the one who's dead, not her. You Dad, I wish you were dead. I wish you were the one that got shot and not her, then we would be happy, then everything would be okay."

Her screams rose over the clanking of the hooves and gravel that carried them closer to their destination and drew a few curious stares.

"I know honey," Aaron said. "Everything you said was right and I'm sorry, and all I can say is that I promise I will do better... I'm sorry."

Rebecca's screams were short-lived, after those words and the defeat she saw on her father's face, her yells quieted to a stream of tears. The water poured from her eyes, mixing with what ran from her nose. Feeling so tired, it hurt to move; she wiped it away with the back of her hands.

"Ew, gross," Eli said.

"Shut up. Leave me alone. Go back to doing whatever it is that you're doing in that little head of yours."

"Dad, she just told me to shut up, and she's been yelling all this time. Tell her to be quiet," Eli said to his dad.

"Rebecca, you do need to keep it down. If someone over-hears you, you know what that means for us." Aaron couldn't say much else, at least not about what Rebecca said. What could he possibly say? That she was right, that he was a loser, a disappointment, a gambler, a drunk, a poor father? That he had killed the woman he loved? She was right, every word, and every sentence. He had blown every opportunity he ever had in his entire life. That's what he did.

He had such promise as a child, the top of his class in school. He wasn't just smart. He was brilliant. His teachers knew he was going to get accepted into the best schools and have it paid for, but like everything else in his life, he screwed it up. He took every shiny new opportunity, and found a way to mess up even the easiest sure thing, and his full scholarship at the University of Pennsylvania -- lost. His first job after finishing -- lost his second job after finishing high school -- lost. All of them went to pieces. That's when he started drinking and after all his failures, they had ended up here.

Running for their lives and hiding out in a tiny hamlet called Faith's Creek. What did he know about the Amish? How could he ask his children to live like this? Again and again, he had tried to think of another way but he could not find one. If they wanted to stay alive, they had to live here. With no electricity, no computers, and no cars for at least a year. His children had lost their mother and now they had lost their friends and their life-style, all because of him.

There was nothing he could say to his daughter, his beautiful Christy... *No, call her Rebecca.* There was nothing he could say to Rebecca... because she was right.

Read all 30 books in the Cherished Love Collection here

ALSO BY SARAH MILLER

All my books are FREE on Kindle Unlimited

If you love Amish Romance, the sweet, clean stories of Sarah Miller receive free stories and join me for the latest news on upcoming books here

These are some of my reader favorites:

5 Amish Brothers

The Amish Faith and Family Collection

Find all Sarah's books on Amazon and click the yellow follow button

This book is dedicated to the wonderful Amish people and the faithful life that they live.

Go in peace, my friends.

As an independent author, Sarah relies on your support. If you enjoyed this book, please leave a review on Amazon or Goodreads.

All the books are sweet, clean, simple Amish romances, and though many of the characters are in all the books, they are complete stories in their own right.

Made in the USA
Middletown, DE
26 March 2025